LIKE FATHER, LIKE SON?

Seems the Garrison apple hasn't fallen far from the tree. According to a very reliable source, Stephen Garrison fathered a love child that he is not claiming! Sound familiar? Our source says the mother and child are living in a rundown cottage on the outskirts of Miami Beach, and millionaire businessman Stephen—who was accompanied by an A-list actress on his yacht just last weekend—hasn't attempted to see his progeny.

In other Garrison news, we hear there may be some new additions to the family. Anna Garrison, the newly minted wife of Garrison honcho Parker, was spotted looking at baby clothes on Lincoln Road Mall. A salesperson mentioned one of the Garrison twins had also picked up several items, but she couldn't distinguish Brooke from Brittany, and the transaction was made in cash. Which one of the Garrison ladies is expecting…or could it be all three?

Dear Reader,

I love writing about intelligent, resourceful, strong women, and Megan Simmons, the heroine of this book, is no exception. Megan's trying to hold her life all together—the child, the job, the family move—until Stephen Garrison walks back into it.

To say these two have been dancing around each other for a long time is the least of it! Stephen owns *the* trendy hotel in South Beach, and now he's out to discover Megan's secrets.

Have you ever had a hotel stay that made you feel as if you're getting away from it all for a while? Now imagine getting involved with a guy who knows how to provide you with that kind of luxurious pampering all the time. I hope you enjoy!

Wishing you the best,

Anna

ANNA DePALO

MILLIONAIRE'S WEDDING REVENGE

Silhouette® Desire

Published by Silhouette Books

America's Publisher of Contemporary Romance

For Susan Crosby and Barbara Daly.
Thanks for the mentoring.

Special thanks and acknowledgment
are given to Anna DePalo
for her contribution to THE GARRISONS miniseries.

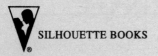

SILHOUETTE BOOKS

ISBN-13: 978-0-373-76819-6
ISBN-10:   0-373-76819-2

MILLIONAIRE'S WEDDING REVENGE

Visit Silhouette Books at www.eHarlequin.com

Printed in U.S.A.

Books by Anna DePalo

Silhouette Desire

Having the Tycoon's Baby #1530
Under the Tycoon's Protection #1643
Tycoon Takes Revenge #1697
Cause for Scandal #1711
Captivated by the Tycoon #1775
An Improper Affair #1803
Millionaire's Wedding Revenge #1819

ANNA DePALO

discovered she was a writer at heart when she realized most people don't walk around with a full cast of characters in their heads. She has lived in Italy and England; she learned to speak French, graduated from Harvard, earned graduate degrees in political science and law, forgotten how to speak French and married her own dashing hero.

A former intellectual property attorney, Anna lives with her husband and son in New York City. Her books have consistently hit the Waldenbooks bestseller list and Nielsen BookScan's list of Top 100 bestselling romances. Her books have won a *Romantic Times BOOKreviews* Reviewers' Choice Award for Best First Series Romance, and have been published in over a dozen countries. Readers are invited to surf to www.desireauthors.com and can also visit Anna at www.annadepalo.com.

THE GARRISONS

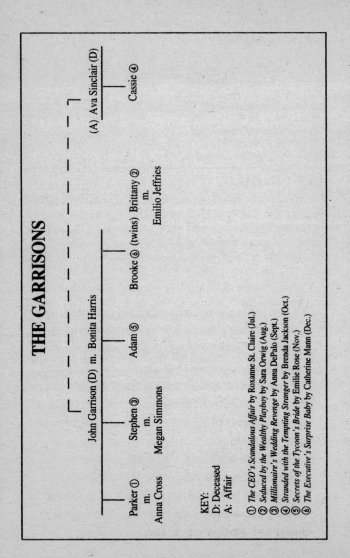

John Garrison (D) m. Bonita Harris

- - - - - - - - (A) Ava Sinclair (D)

Parker ①   Stephen ③   Adam ⑤   Brooke ⑥ (twins) Brittany ②   Cassie ④
m.   m.   m.
Anna Cross   Megan Simmons   Emilio Jeffries

KEY:
D: Deceased
A: Affair

① *The CEO's Scandalous Affair by Roxanne St. Claire (Jul.)*
② *Seduced by the Wealthy Playboy by Sara Orwig (Aug.)*
③ *Millionaire's Wedding Revenge by Anna DePalo (Sept.)*
④ *Stranded with the Tempting Stranger by Brenda Jackson (Oct.)*
⑤ *Secrets of the Tycoon's Bride by Emilie Rose (Nov.)*
⑥ *The Executive's Surprise Baby by Catherine Mann (Dec.)*

One

When Megan Simmons left Miami four years ago, she'd struggled every day to regain her equilibrium and put the past behind her. But her equilibrium had eluded her, and the past had dogged her every step.

Now, at the sound of the knock on her open office door, she glanced up from the documents on her desk and into the eyes of the man she'd once thought she'd never see again.

Her breath left her in a whoosh.

She put down the papers she was holding.

"Your new partner is hard at work already, Conrad."

His voice went through her like fine cognac. It *always* had. Particularly in bed.

This time, though, she immediately sensed the danger. Stephen's words held a note of cynical amusement.

Her eyes traveled to the second man at her door. Conrad Elkind's offer of partnership in the interior design firm she used to work for as an employee was the reason she was back in Miami.

"Good news, Megan," Conrad said heartily. "We've got an assignment to redesign part of the Garrison Grand. Stephen here was so impressed by the job you did on the Garrison, Inc. building four years ago that he requested you work on this new project."

Her eyes shot back to Stephen. From the look on his face, she knew this was no mere coincidence.

Stephen's lips twisted. "I asked Conrad not to let the cat out of the bag until we'd sealed the deal."

She felt the blood drain from her face. If she hadn't already been sitting down in a chair, she'd have collapsed into one.

When she'd moved back to Miami, she'd known she might run into Stephen, but she hadn't expected to be working for him within weeks of being back at her old firm.

Someday, in the not too distant future, she hoped to be a *senior* partner. Her firm would be Elkind, Ross, Gardner & *Simmons*. Now, however, Stephen loomed like an immovable obstacle in that path.

She composed herself and stood, even as her eyes

shot daggers at the man who'd haunted her days and not too few of her nights.

"What an *unexpected* compliment," she announced as she came around her desk.

She was dressed in a sand-colored skirt suit paired with an emerald blouse that echoed the color of her eyes. She was glad now for the professional armor, though—in a nod to the hot, sunny weather—her feet were encased in strappy tan sandals.

The end of summer in Miami was still *hot*. The September sun radiated outside Elkind, Ross & Gardner's cool offices, and its rays filtered through the blinds on her office window, hitting her back.

Still, though her sandals lent another two inches to her five-foot-nine frame, the boost wasn't enough to counteract Stephen's intimidating presence. At six foot three, he loomed over her, radiating a charisma and sex appeal that were palpable.

He was the epitome of tall, dark and handsome, with jet-black hair and coffee eyes, and a body that looked as if it would make military basic training seem no more rigorous than a stroll in the park.

She'd seen evidence of his effect on women four years ago. They'd *swooned* over him. *She'd* been stupid enough to swoon over him, too.

Even now, she felt a tingling that went all over.

She wondered whether it was the cleft chin—a Garrison family trait—that did it for some women.

But unlike screen idol Cary Grant, Stephen was a living, breathing playboy nonpareil.

A quick glance at his left hand was enough for her to confirm he was still single.

Conrad glanced at his watch. "I've got a phone conference starting in five minutes, so I'm going to leave the two of you to talk and get reacquainted."

Getting reacquainted was the last thing she wanted to do with Stephen Garrison, ever, but she forced herself to nod. "Thanks, Conrad."

When the older partner had retreated, her gaze came back to Stephen, and of its own volition, her chin rose a fraction.

Then she caught herself. It was ridiculous for her to feel defensive. *She* had nothing to feel defensive about.

"Hello, Stephen. Won't you have a seat?" She turned to head back to her desk. "I'm sure we can help you with whatever it is you're looking for."

"That's what I'm counting on," he said silkily.

She heard him close the office door, and she couldn't help but think of the sound as the opening bell in a boxing match.

She turned to face him. "I suppose it's too much to hope that your appearance here today is a mere coincidence."

"You guessed right," he drawled. "It's taken a while, but I plan to get the answers I'm looking for."

"Why do I get the impression we're not talking about the Garrison Grand?"

"Four years ago, you left Miami without a backward glance."

"You mean I left *you*."

A muscle jumped in his jaw.

"No one leaves a Garrison, is that it?" she said, hands braced on hips. Hips that now had experienced childbirth.

Motherhood had instilled in her a newfound courage, changing her from the woman she'd been four years ago. She'd do anything to make sure her daughter had the future she deserved, including struggling with the demands of single parenthood.

Including coming back to Miami.

Last month, she'd uprooted herself and Jade from her hometown of Indianapolis, and returned to Miami, though she knew it was the Garrisons' town. She'd been lured by the promise of a lucrative junior partnership in her old design firm.

Now, looking more closely at Stephen, she realized the intervening years had wrought a change in him, too. She knew he was thirty-one now, only a year older than she was, but he had a physical maturity he hadn't possessed the last time she'd seen him.

It wasn't that he looked different. He was still as good-looking as ever.

It was more that he wore his power more easily.

His air of command had lost its harsh shine and achieved a subtle luster.

Subtle, but more dangerous, she reminded herself. With that thought, she blurted, "How did you know I was back in town?"

He shoved his hands in the pockets of his bespoke suit and sauntered closer, completely comfortable in an office that should have been her domain.

She thanked her lucky stars that she hadn't set out any photos or revealing mementos. She also prayed Conrad hadn't mentioned anything too revealing about her private life.

"How did I know you were back in Miami?" he repeated, as if taking his time to consider her words. "Now that's the central question, isn't it?"

For all his smoothness, she couldn't miss the quiet danger in his voice.

His eyes held hers, and she felt as if she were drowning in their dark depths. "It seems you never mentioned to your friend Anna that you and I used to be lovers."

Oh, Anna, Megan wailed silently. Why, oh why, did you have to mention me to Stephen Garrison?

Yet, she could hardly blame her friend. She'd kept Anna in the dark—she'd kept *everyone* in the dark— about the debacle in her life four years ago.

Stephen's lips twisted sardonically. "If you wanted your return to Miami to remain a secret, you should have sewn up that hole with the brand-new Mrs. Parker Garrison."

He was right, of course, but it didn't make the pill any easier to swallow.

"You know, it's funny," Stephen went on, his tone implying it was anything but humorous, "there we were sitting around Sunday dinner at my parents' estate in Bal Harbour a few weeks ago when I happened to mention I was looking for an interior design firm to update the Garrison Grand." He paused. "One guess as to what Anna said."

Megan compressed her lips, but Stephen apparently wasn't looking for a response.

"She mentioned her friend Megan Simmons had just moved back to Miami to be a partner at Elkind, Ross." Stephen rubbed his jaw, then paused as his eyes focused on her again. "I didn't even know you and Anna were friends."

"That's how Anna got her start at Garrison, Inc. four years ago," she said tightly. "I'd gotten to know people in the HR department at Garrison headquarters when I was working on the redesign there, and I recommended her for a job. She was ready to leave Indianapolis."

She braced her fingertips against the top of her desk. Her legs felt rubbery, but since Stephen had yet to mention Jade, she guessed Anna had left out she had a daughter now.

"Right," Stephen said, sauntering even closer. "Four years ago would be right about the time you skipped town."

"I *decided* to leave Miami, yes." She'd *fled,* but these days she'd learned when to run and when to stand her ground.

"Of course," Stephen went on, seeming not to have heard her, "if you hadn't run off like a scared rabbit when I headed your way at Anna and Parker's wedding reception recently, we could have had this conversation elsewhere."

She'd hoped he hadn't spotted her mingling among the guests at Anna and Parker's lavish beach wedding, but clearly it had been a false hope despite her quick departure.

Her fear of coming face-to-face with him had almost kept her from attending, even without Jade, but loyalty to Anna had ultimately won out.

Still, she wasn't about to concede an inch. "I did *not* run away."

He quirked a brow disbelievingly.

"I just refused to sully Anna and Parker's wedding day with an unpleasant conversation."

He laughed humorlessly. "Spare me the drama."

"Is it so hard to believe there are women who don't want to flirt with you?" she retorted, her temper igniting.

"I haven't found any who've turned down an invitation to my bed, sweetheart," he shot back. "Including *you*."

"Yes, but I was the one who ultimately walked away," she countered, then went on the offensive. "Does it bother you, Stephen? Did I ruin your perfect record with women when I dumped you?"

A muscle ticked in his jaw.

She tilted her head. "You know, I promise not to tell…."

His eyes narrowed, his lips becoming a thin line, and for a moment, she worried she'd gone too far.

They'd always been good at pressing each other's buttons. It was what had added an element of exhilarating excitement to their short-lived affair.

She reminded herself, however, that nothing *she* could do now could match *his* betrayal at the end of their affair.

He searched her face. "Did you run because I was getting under your skin?" he mused, his voice lowering. "Were things getting too hot in the bedroom for you? Was your cool facade in danger of melting?"

She sucked in a breath.

"You know it was good," he murmured.

"Don't flatter yourself!"

She hadn't wanted an ugly confrontation four years ago, so she'd walked away without an explanation—without a goodbye. She'd been afraid that if she faced him with her knowledge of his betrayal, he'd convince her to stay.

Because she knew she was weak where he was concerned. Because she was intimately acquainted with just how charmingly persuasive he could be.

He shifted a step back suddenly, laying off some of the pressure. "Why did you leave?" he asked bluntly.

"I told you in the last conversation—"

"A phone message."

"I wanted a clean break," she lied again.

"After dodging my calls for days," he accused.

"You were out of town on business."

"Yeah, and then you were—supposedly."

"I was never good at breaking up," she countered, "and it was clear to me our fling was coming to an end."

As clear as the woman whom she'd seen leaving his yacht, she added silently.

His jaw clenched. Evidently, he didn't like her response, but he also wasn't going to dispute her belief.

She read his silence as confirmation, and her stomach dropped sickeningly. Obviously, if she hadn't called it quits first, Stephen would soon have been giving her his "it was good while it lasted, babe" talk.

"There, that wasn't so bad, was it?" he taunted finally. "A simple explanation for why you ended the affair. You could have given it to me at Anna's wedding without an ugly scene."

Perversely, she felt her temper rise again. "Are

you suggesting that if you'd had a chance to talk to me before now, you wouldn't be here today with a brand-new project for Elkind, Ross?" she demanded. "Because if so, I don't believe it. I know you too well, Stephen."

"You *used to* know me well, sweetheart," he responded silkily. "About as well as any woman who's shared my bed."

She was just one in a crowd, Megan thought bitterly. *As if she could ever forget.*

Yet one more reason Stephen must never, *ever,* know about Jade.

She could bear working for him if she had to. She just couldn't bear having him jeopardize what mattered most.

Stephen stared at the woman who'd walked away from him four years ago without a second glance.

He'd wanted her from the moment he'd seen her, coming out of a conference room at Garrison, Inc., right after her firm had inked a deal with his older brother, Parker, to refurbish the offices at Garrison headquarters.

She'd been laughing at something Parker had said, and the laugh, combined with everything else, had hit him like fine aged whiskey burning a path to an empty stomach.

She'd been intoxicating. A tall redhead with legs

that went on forever, and a body that was all curves. A Jessica Rabbit come to life in all her bombshell glory.

He'd pictured her beneath him in bed, those long legs wrapped around him as he lost himself inside her.

And the reality had lived up to the billing—for the first time in his jaded experience with women.

Their five-month affair had been explosive. They'd spent weekends aboard his yacht, just enjoying each other, then had sneaked away in the middle of the workday for lunchtime sex in a hotel room.

Fortunately, he'd owned—and still did—the most luxurious hotel in Miami's trendy South Beach, and he kept a private suite there for his own use.

On days when he was done meeting and greeting the high-rolling hotel guests who'd come to frolic in the sun and party in nearby nightclubs, and he didn't feel like heading back to his four-bedroom villa and estate near South Beach, he could crash at the hotel.

This particular day, however, was supposed to be about putting a coda on unfinished business. Instead, he was irritated to discover, she still had as much an effect on him as ever.

The urge to touch her was irresistible, despite the fact that *she* had chosen to end their affair four years ago with a curt phone message.

He'd tried to contact her, always getting her voice mail, until he'd discovered from the receptionist at her design firm that Megan had given two weeks' notice and skipped town to go back home to Indianapolis.

To hell with it, he'd decided. His male pride had been stung, and he'd already put it on the line enough by breaking his cardinal rule: don't look back.

He'd never been dumped before. He was used to leaving women, not having women leave him. His breakup with Megan had been the first time he'd experienced being cast aside, and he hadn't liked it.

"Why are you here?" Megan demanded now, her green eyes flashing.

To get some answers, and as it happens, I need to hire an interior designer. He'd figured he'd enjoy having Megan on his payroll, playing it until he got some answers, and in the meantime, keeping the pressure on—letting her see just what she'd walked away from.

Now, he shrugged. "Isn't it obvious? I need an interior designer to update the look of the Garrison Grand. Your firm has done work on various Garrison properties in the past, including the Garrison Grand."

"Why ask for me?" She gestured around her. "Any number of people in this office could help you."

Because I'm going to enjoy seducing you back into my bed. "Because you're one of the best interior designers in town, and you're the one who's most familiar with the Garrison account."

He hadn't shown up with the intention of reigniting their affair, but now he'd seen her again, the idea appealed increasingly.

Her response as to why she'd ended their relationship had been only a little more satisfying than the one she'd given him by phone, and he wasn't sure he bought it: their affair had been so hot, he thought his fingers would be singed.

Now that she was back in town—and back in his orbit, by his own doing—he intended to dig a little deeper.

Conrad had told him he and the other partners had lured Meghan back to the firm. They needed new blood, and she was that good.

Megan opened and closed her mouth. "But we—"

"—slept together?" he finished for her.

At her indrawn breath, he arched a brow. "You have a problem working for former lovers?"

"This is the first time I've had to face the situation!"

"What? Worried about maintaining your professionalism?"

"It's not *my* professionalism I'm worried about," she retorted.

He swept her a look, letting his gaze linger on her chest before coming back to meet her mutinous gaze.

He smiled slowly. "Then you have nothing to worry about."

She raised her chin. "I'll ask that someone else be assigned to work on the Garrison Grand."

"Careful, sweetheart. The Garrison property is one of the most lucrative accounts your firm has going. You wouldn't want to be the one who caused your firm to lose it."

Her eyes widened, and color seeped into her face, masking the dusting of freckles there—freckles that he'd spent one memorable night kissing, one by one.

"You wouldn't dare," she gritted.

He shrugged. "Since you're just back in the office, I'm assuming you've got the most time to devote to a new account. You're going to find it hard to explain to your partners why you can't."

Her shoulders heaved, and her lips compressed.

"Fine," she said finally.

He looked back at her blandly.

"But our relationship this time is strictly business."

He inclined his head. "Whatever you say…Meggi-kins."

He was going to enjoy coaxing Megan Simmons back into his bed. And this time, she'd leave only when he asked her to.

Two

Megan stepped past the liveried doorman and into the cool lobby of the Garrison Grand.

The change was a welcome respite from the heat outside. She'd dressed for the hot weather in a lime-green sheath dress with a short matching jacket, her feet encased in strappy sandals.

A couple of men sent appreciative looks her way.

She knew that as a tall redhead in heels, she was hard to overlook—even if she wore her hair tied back and constrained, as it was today.

What she *wasn't* used to, she thought, as she looked around at the hotel guests in the lobby, was the cool sophistication of Stephen's world.

She'd almost forgotten what this world was like, having spent the past few years variously wiping baby food off her shirt, reading nursery rhymes and teaching Jade how to use the potty.

Now though, as she surveyed the women with lithe tanned bodies dressed in halter tops or less, and the men projecting a chic style in khakis and designer shirts, she knew she had to gird herself for today's meeting.

Glancing to her left, she noticed Stephen walking toward her from across the lobby.

She watched as he was waylaid by an employee, then as his progress was halted again by someone who appeared to be a familiar hotel guest.

When he finally approached, she said, "I thought I was meeting one of your executives."

"Change of plans," he said, cupping her elbow and gently steering her with a subtle pressure.

He slanted her a look. "That is, unless you *mind* it's me."

"No," she responded automatically. Since she had been the one to call their relationship strictly professional, she had no choice but to stick to the script. "Of course I don't care."

Of course I care. Just being in the same room with him was enough to make her tense and jittery.

As it was, little shock waves coursed through her from the casual contact of his hand at her elbow.

They walked across the majestic soaring lobby

toward the elevators. One end of the lobby led to the street, and the other end, with columns alternating with billowing white curtains, opened onto the Garrison Grand's private beach. The smell of surf and sand wafted in.

She hadn't been able to stop herself over the years from reading the occasional news article about Stephen and the Garrison Grand. The hotel had kept a fantastic reputation while she and Stephen had been dating, but it had surpassed itself since then, becoming the *it* place for the rich and famous who flocked to South Beach.

Walking through the lobby now, she could understand why. Stephen seemed to keep everything new and cutting edge.

"I'm looking to redesign some of the meeting rooms on the second floor," Stephen said. "Then we can talk about other changes—what else needs to be revamped and updated."

His deep voice buffeted her like the warm jets of a hot tub.

This is not going to work, she thought. How could she stand to work with him when she couldn't even think straight?

Yet, she had no choice. After Stephen had left her office yesterday, she'd gone to see Conrad. The meeting had confirmed everything Stephen had said: everyone else in the office was too busy with other projects to be the lead person on the Garrison Grand, and they were looking to her to be a team player.

Now, as Stephen called the elevator and they rode up together, she felt the air between them fairly crackle with tension.

When they stepped out on the second floor, they walked down a hallway with recessed lighting along either side of its carpeted floor.

He gave her a quick tour of the business center and various conference rooms. They ended up at the end of the hall, where Stephen opened a set of double doors and ushered her inside the last empty conference room.

As she walked past him, she was careful not to brush against him. She didn't think she could stand it.

This conference room contained a long, rectangular, glass-topped table that looked as if it could seat twenty. Like the others, the decor was modern, with high-backed office chairs and all the proper business amenities: phones, a flat-screen television with a DVD player, and a projection screen that appeared as if it was normally hidden behind a wooden wall panel.

"I find it hard to believe," she observed after looking around and turning back to Stephen, "that anyone can work in paradise's playground."

It was a thought that had increasingly hit her during their brief tour.

A smile slashed across Stephen's face. "*I* do," he

said, then added drily, "That's why you can't see the beach from this room or the others."

She walked farther into the room, trailing her fingertips along the top of the table before setting her purse down, putting together the thoughts and ideas that had been formulating since the beginning of their tour.

He watched her.

"Very modern," she mused.

"Very," he agreed, "but I'm not looking for merely modern. I want different—unique—and that means changing to stay ahead of our competitors."

She turned to face him. "Are you thinking of the Hotel Victoria?"

"Just back in town, and you've heard of it already," he quipped.

She lifted her shoulders. "I'm an interior designer. Of course I'm interested in news of a hotel opening."

"Well, don't be too impressed," he advised. "Jordan Jefferies is an imitator, not an innovator, and I'm more than ready for a fight."

Stephen's comments reminded her of everything she knew about him from four years ago. He was still strong-willed, powerful and competitive.

Seeking to change the direction of the conversation, she said, "The conference rooms are different from the rest of the hotel. They don't have the same white theme—"

His lips quirked. "We were looking for something a little more professional for the business rooms. White is the ultimate indulgence."

"Decadent luxury," she agreed.

It was what his celebrity guests came for. She could only imagine what his cleaning bill amounted to for the hotel. She knew most of the guest rooms were decorated in white, with splashes of color lent mostly by fresh flowers and marble accents.

But then again, given the room rate at the Garrison Grand, she could well imagine Stephen seeing healthy profits.

She thought about the suite at the hotel that Stephen kept for his personal use. It had also been done in white, she recollected. But unlike the other suites in the hotel, the room rate there had been a night of passion in Stephen's bed.

She felt herself heat at the thought.

"What are you thinking?" he said, and she jumped.

"I was just mulling the possibilities," she said quickly, trying to cover her lapse. "It occurred to me to do a takeoff on the decor in the rest of the hotel. White and dark blue. White leather, midnight-blue velvet. Different textures, different fabrics."

She spoke rapidly, sketching her idea for him, the thoughts spilling from her. "White to echo the calming relaxation of the rest of the hotel, midnight-blue for business. Navy is a business color, but we'll subtly undermine it by casting it in sinful velvet and giving it a unique hue."

His long-ago familiar lopsided smile appeared. "Tell me more."

It was easy to think *sinful* in his presence, she wanted to tell him.

Her heart beat rapidly.

There was a time, four years ago, when they'd been so hot for each other, they'd have abandoned their business meeting to sneak away upstairs and have frantic sex in his hotel suite, kissing and holding hands in the elevator as soon as the doors closed.

Or he'd have locked the door, and taken her right here.

Not anymore.

And she shouldn't be having such lascivious thoughts about a client, she reminded herself. Particularly him. She was mommy material now.

She glanced around. "We'll replace the wood paneling with sound-soak material to help with the acoustics and lighting. It comes in an off-white color, but with a suede finish, so it'll blend with the decor."

He smiled. "Sounds good."

"It'll sound even better when I've had time to draw up plans," she responded as she walked back toward him. "We'll need to move the business center, too. It should be convenient but less obtrusive. Right now, from what I saw, it has too much glass, in my opinion."

"I'm liking it even more," he replied.

"Aren't you lucky, then, that you got me before Jordan Jefferies did?" she joked, then could have bitten off her tongue as Stephen's eyes darkened.

She watched as his gaze traveled over her. "Yeah, I *got* you," he drawled before he met her gaze. "The question is, when will I have you again?"

Her stomach flipped. *"Never."*

"Never is a long time, sweetheart."

"I thought we agreed to keep this relationship strictly professional."

"We did?" he murmured.

"That would put sexual innuendo on the wrong side of the line," she informed him.

"How about dinner?" he asked, his voice flippant even as his look heated her all over. "Would having dinner together be on the wrong side of the line?"

"Mo—" She stopped to clear the catch in her throat. "Most definitely."

"Too bad," he murmured.

Yes, too bad. Then she caught herself.

No, not too bad. He was lying, cheating vermin, and she'd be three kinds of fool to fall under the spell of his seductive charm—again. What was wrong with her?

He looked at her hair. "Why is your hair up?"

"It's hot."

Outside. It's hot outside. But she felt as if she was burning up right in here.

Before she could stop him, he reached up, and with an efficient move, released the barrette holding her hair in place.

A cascade of dark red hair followed.

"Much better," he remarked. "I always liked it better down."

"Stop it." She didn't know whom she was angrier with, him for putting the moves on her, or herself for her breathless reaction.

"It was good four years ago," he stated.

"Yes, and it's over now."

"Easily rectified. Have dinner with me."

Stephen being Stephen, it was more a command than a request.

"I can't. I need to go—"

She clamped her mouth shut. He'd gotten her so discombobulated, she'd almost said she had to go relieve the babysitter. It was an excuse that came effortlessly to her lips. She'd grown accustomed to using it over the past three years.

"You have to go, what?" he asked.

"Nothing," she responded. "When I have something down on paper for this project, I'll call you."

Then she grabbed her purse and brushed past him in her haste to get out of the room.

Stephen stood looking out his office window, his suit jacket hanging open and bunched above the hands shoved in his pockets. He had a rare moment for calm introspection.

He'd come on strong with Megan earlier. Maybe too strong, he admitted to himself now.

She'd reacted like a deer caught in headlights. It was far different from the way she'd reacted to his pursuit four years ago. Then she'd flatly refused to go out with him, but the unaccustomed taste of rejection had simply spiked his interest.

He'd made up reasons to show up at Garrison, Inc. headquarters, even recruiting Parker so he would know when Megan was due to show up there.

He'd engaged her in casual conversation, and eventually discovered they'd both been captains of their high school swim teams and they were both football fans, though she followed her hometown Indianapolis Colts while he was a Miami Dolphins fan.

More importantly, he'd liked the fact she was ambitious without taking herself too seriously. It was something he could relate to.

He'd discovered she'd left her home in Indiana and come down to Florida because of the career opportunities in the interior design field. She dealt with the aesthetics of workplace and hospitality environments, while his aim was to make his hotel the premier accommodation in Miami by focusing on cutting-edge design.

To his chagrin, he'd also discovered his reputation

as a player had preceded him and Megan was understandably wary.

"Why won't you go out with me?" he'd asked her one day, bestowing one of his trademark killer smiles. He'd found from experience that the direct approach often worked best. "It's been rumored I'm actually a reasonable dinner partner, decent arm candy and even a fairly good kisser."

Her lips had twitched. "Yes, and that's not *all* apparently. I know about your reputation."

"Rumors of my prowess have been exaggerated," he parried, not averse to shamelessly self-serving comments.

She laughed. "Can I quote you? It's rare to hear a guy like you argue for once that his image has outstripped the reality. Still, I noticed you didn't say *greatly* exaggerated."

"A guy like me?" he repeated, pretending to look wounded.

"Mmm-hmm. Exactly like you," she said archly, turning back to her work.

Still, he'd eventually caught her at a weak moment one day and coaxed her into having an overdue lunch with him at a corner bistro. She'd relented, and their affair had taken off from there.

Yet, back then she'd never had that apprehensive quality around him that she'd exhibited earlier today.

People changed, of course, but he wondered what could have triggered it in this case.

Still, he didn't intend to let the pressure off Megan. He wanted her—sooner rather than later.

Three

When Stephen showed up at her office two days later, Megan was prepared to act as if their encounter in the Garrison Grand's conference room had never happened.

She gritted her teeth now as she led the way down the hall to Elkind, Ross's storage rooms, where they kept fabrics, carpets and wall coverings.

She was determined to keep this an all-business relationship even if it killed her.

She could feel his presence behind her—authoritative, confident, all male—and wished now she'd worn something more severe than a wrap dress and heels to work today.

They stepped into the secluded and very empty storage room, and Megan couldn't help thinking that there were some requirements of her job that she could easily do without right now.

Stephen looked around at the shelves surrounding them. They were all piled high with materials.

"So this is what things really look like around here," he said, his voice tinged with amusement. "I was beginning to think, judging from your austere office, that this was a place where even a paper clip wouldn't dare to be out of place."

"I haven't had a chance to settle in yet," she responded.

Let him think what he liked, she thought. She didn't want him getting any hints of her life as it was now.

She walked toward the back of the room to search for the samples she was looking for, and he followed, then stopped beside her. In his dark pinstripe suit, he pulled off the look of restrained power effortlessly.

Retrieving a small chip from a cardboard box, she said, "This is a sample of the type of wall covering I'd like to use in the conference rooms."

As he took the chip from her, their hands brushed, sending awareness shooting through her.

"As you can see," she went on, determined to ignore the sensation, "it's not quite white, but close enough, I think."

"Right," he muttered, but his eyes were focused on her, not the sample in his hand.

She scooted over to another shelf. "And these are examples of the fabrics I'd like to use. This is the white leather—" she tapped a bolt of fabric "—and this is the midnight velvet."

She watched him feel the leather, his tanned hands dark against the lightness of the fabric, and an erotic charge went through her.

Cursing her wayward mind, and seeking to distract both him and herself, she yanked the bolt of velvet fabric forward with more force than necessary.

"As you can see, the color has a depth and a richness to it that make it more than merely navy-blue. It's plush, and at the same time, fairly easy to clean thanks to the wonders of new industrial processes."

He reached out and touched the fabric, his hand slowly stroking over it.

She nearly gulped. It was impossible, she belatedly realized, to have this conversation *without* a sexual subtext.

"You're right," he said, gazing directly at her. "It's…sinful."

She could see amusement lurking in his eyes. Damn him. He knew exactly the effect this conversation was having on her.

The sudden ring of a phone made her jump and broke the spell.

Stephen arched a brow.

"We keep a phone in the supply room," she explained, hurrying over to a nearby cabinet, "in case anyone needs to be reached while they're working."

While they're being seduced by the look in a client's eyes.

Picking up the phone, she said, "Hello?"

"Megan, it's Tiffany."

What a time for her babysitter to call! Maybe it hadn't been such a great idea to tell her secretary to forward any important calls. She cast an involuntary look at Stephen from the corner of her eyes.

"Is anything wrong?" she asked.

"Just checking in."

She groaned inwardly. "Thanks. That's thoughtful."

"Jade wants to go to the park," Tiffany continued, "so we might not be here when you arrive home. I didn't want you to worry, so I thought I'd call now. If we don't beat you back, we'll be on the way."

"That's fine."

"We might stop for some ice cream."

"Just remember what she's allergic to," she responded in a lowered voice.

"Will do."

When she hung up, Stephen asked, "Is everything okay? I heard you mention the word *allergic.*"

She thought frantically, even as she struggled to appear composed.

"Ah, it's a client I'm taking to lunch," she fibbed. "I was just reminding my secretary to bear in mind what the client is allergic to when making reservations." She waved her hand around. "You know, ah, ethnic cuisine and all."

"Right."

She cleared her throat. Time to get out of the pressure cooker that the storage room had turned into. "If you follow me back to my office, we can consider the layout of the Garrison Grand redesign in greater detail."

What was Megan hiding? She'd appeared furtive when speaking on the phone in the storage room earlier in the day.

Stephen stared out the window of his office, his fingers steepled, his feet crossed on his desk.

He knew she wasn't married. She didn't wear a ring, and he figured Megan would be one to change her surname when she got married.

Maybe there was a boyfriend in the picture.

His lips thinned at the thought of Megan with another man. Still, her reaction to his asking for a date *hadn't* been to say she was seeing someone. She'd been about to say something, but he was fairly sure it wasn't that. She would have finished her thought otherwise, because a steady boyfriend would have afforded her an easy excuse to turn him down.

Still, he wondered how many lovers she'd had since their breakup. He'd hardly been celibate himself. They're were plenty of beautiful women in South Beach who were only too happy to hook up with the wealthy and good-looking owner of one of the trendiest places in town.

But none of those relationships had gone as deep as the one with Megan. When his mind had slipped its leash and he'd compared those women to her, they'd come up short.

He thought back to Megan's accusation. *No one leaves a Garrison.*

Yeah, it had irked him to be dumped. Particularly since, as far as he was concerned, their relationship had been just fine. The sex had been great, and she'd challenged and fascinated him out of bed, too.

She was the one woman he'd actually given thought to settling down with.

"You look severe."

He looked at his open office door and noticed his new sister-in-law, Anna, holding on to the doorjamb.

He pushed away from his desk and lowered his feet.

Anna walked into the room. "What were you thinking? I could practically see the storm clouds."

"Nothing," he said, standing. "What brings you to the Garrison Grand?"

He kept his personal life private, including the particulars of his short-lived affair with Megan.

Still, now he knew Anna and Megan were friends, he figured his new sister-in-law could be useful to him. He wasn't averse to doing some subtle digging.

"Parker and I are having dinner at the Opalesce Room," Anna responded.

He flashed a smile that more than one woman had characterized as devilish. "Come to invite me along?"

Anna laughed. "Hardly. Parker and I are still honeymooners."

"Yeah, how can any of us forget?"

The change in his brother had been extraordinary. The guy actually seemed to be in love, which—given the train wreck their own parents' marriage had been until their father had died—was some feat. It also spoke volumes about the woman before him.

His parents' marriage had been marred by Bonita Garrison's drinking. Still, after John Garrison's sudden death from a heart attack, everyone had been shocked to learn he'd fathered a love child.

"Actually," Anna went on, "since your brother is going to be late, I thought I'd stop by on the off chance that Megan might be around. I know she's working on the business center renovation."

"She came by yesterday." He didn't add she'd hightailed it out of there after his thwarted pass.

Anna looked momentarily disappointed, then

shrugged. "Oh, well. I suppose I'll catch up with her soon." After a moment, she added impetuously, "I'm glad you hired her."

"Yeah," he said, coming around his desk, "I didn't know until you mentioned it that you were close friends with one of Miami's best up-and-coming designers."

"In fact," Anna admitted, "I have Megan to thank for my start at Garrison, Inc. four years ago. She'd gotten to know people in the HR department while she worked on renovations at Garrison headquarters."

"So she said. What are friends for?" he remarked flippantly as he made his way to a side cabinet that held a small refrigerator and beverages.

Recently he'd suspected Anna of corporate espionage, but he'd been proved wrong. Someone, though, *was* leaking secrets to the damn Jefferies brothers. Last month, editorial coverage and a photo spread in *Luxury Traveler* that he'd been working hard to negotiate for the Garrison Grand had somehow fallen through, and the magazine had instead—by strange coincidence—decided to profile Jordan Jefferies's soon-to-be-opened Hotel Victoria.

Fortunately, Parker had asked the family's private investigator, Ace Martin, to ferret out the traitor. It didn't help matters, though, that one of his younger twin sisters had just decided to get herself engaged to Emilio Jefferies.

"Drink?" he offered.

"No, thanks. Parker should be here any minute."

Stephen poured himself some bottled water. After watching his mother drink herself silly, he was careful with the heavy stuff.

"Anyway, I'm glad you hired Megan after I mentioned her for the project here at the hotel," Anna continued. "I'm glad I was able to return the favor she did for me."

"I'm sure she can't thank you enough," he responded tongue-in-cheek, thinking of Megan's reaction when he'd shown up in her office.

"I also convinced her to take over the cute little house I was leasing in Coral Gables."

He turned back toward Anna, and took a sip of his drink. "You don't say?"

Parker appeared in the doorway behind his wife, and Anna turned.

"Great, you're not as late as I thought you'd be," Anna said.

Parker gave his wife a quick kiss.

"Leave it for dessert," Stephen said to no one in particular.

Parker flashed him a grin, and Anna looked embarrassed.

Stephen raised his glass in salute. "Enjoy your meal."

Thanks to Anna, he had more important matters to attend to, starting with calling over to HR at Garrison headquarters and finding out his sister-in-law's old address.

Four

He scanned the house numbers, and when he found the modest little home in Coral Gables, he pulled up at the curb and parked his Aston Martin convertible.

As Stephen strode up the well-kept front lawn, he scanned the home's facade. It was hard to tell if anyone was home.

The house was painted white, with light blue shutters and trim providing vivid contrast. Flower boxes spilled over from the front windows, and some small bushes dotted the lawn before them.

He pocketed his sunglasses before finding and ringing the doorbell.

It was a late Saturday afternoon, and the temperature hovered modestly in the mideighties. Megan could be anywhere, he thought. She could be out running errands or seeing friends. If she wasn't home, his plan was to try another time.

He rang the doorbell again.

He knew just calling Megan up and asking for a date wouldn't work. She'd already turned down his invitation to dinner.

So, he'd decided to show up on her doorstep unannounced. He figured he could offer his help for what remained to be done moving in, and in the process, he might even persuade her about dinner.

She was bound to be more relaxed outside of work.

On top of it all, he was more than a little curious about what Megan was hiding. At the Garrison Grand the other day, when she'd abruptly cut herself off, the alarmed look that had crossed her face had been telling.

Showing up at her house would give him a good opportunity to discover any secrets.

With that thought, he rang a third time.

After waiting for a few moments, and again receiving no response, he resigned himself to trying again another time.

He turned to leave when a distant laugh suddenly stopped him.

The laugh came again, and this time he thought it was coming from the rear of the house.

Changing direction, he cut across the lawn, then

turned the corner and walked along the concrete path that ran along the side of the house.

As he neared the backyard, he could tell from the sound of movement that there were definitely people outside.

"Mommy, the green."

"Okay, Jade. Just a minute, honey."

He recognized the second voice as Megan's.

Even as his mind roared to life trying to make sense of the conversation—*Megan, a mother*—he turned the corner into the backyard.

His eyes rapidly took in Megan, her back to him, sitting at a plastic picnic table opposite a little girl. They were finger-painting and wearing matching smocks.

The little girl looked up suddenly and stared at him.

He stared back—and felt the breath leave him.

The girl had dark brown hair, pulled back in a ponytail, and her large brown eyes stared at him innocently.

But the characteristic he zeroed in on was her cleft chin.

He was all too familiar with the trait. He viewed it every morning when he shaved, and he saw it in the faces of his siblings.

All the Garrisons had cleft chins.

The girl looked to be around three, which would make her the right age....

His mind froze.

The little girl smiled and pointed. "Mommy, there's a man here."

He watched as Megan looked over her shoulder.

When she saw him, her eyes widened and her lips parted. Color drained from her face.

She owed him some answers big time, Stephen thought grimly.

He could read the truth in Megan's reaction, could see it in his daughter's face. *His daughter.*

"Hello, Megan." Given his fury, he was surprised by how even his voice was.

Not in front of Jade, her eyes seemed to beg him as he stepped forward.

"And who is this pretty girl?" he asked, looking over at Jade.

The little girl giggled. "I'm Jade."

A door opened and slammed. "Sorry, I'm late—"

Stephen turned to see a woman—a cute blonde who looked to be in her early twenties—stopped in front of Megan's back door.

Megan rose. "That's okay, Tiffany. I was just entertaining Jade with some finger-painting."

Stephen noticed Tiffany gazing at him as if she recognized him.

More likely than not, she did. If she and her friends partied at the Garrison Grand or one of the other hot spots among the Garrison properties, chances were good she would have seen him. Or maybe she recognized him from the newspapers.

"My name is Jade, and I like green!"

Despite the charged atmosphere, Stephen couldn't help smiling at the little girl's outburst. The tyke had personality.

Megan looked down at her daughter. "Time to clean up, sweetie."

"But, Mommy, we're not done!"

"Why don't I finish painting with Jade?" Tiffany offered, stepping forward, though her eyes remained on him.

Doubtlessly, Stephen thought, she was wondering what he was doing standing in Megan's yard.

"Yes, Megan," he drawled, "why don't you let Tiffany take over, since you and I *need to talk.*"

His tone said she wasn't getting rid of him. He wanted answers *now*.

Their eyes met and clashed until Megan broke contact.

"All right," she said finally, then raised her arms to untie the smock from behind her neck.

Because Tiffany continued to look at him curiously, he said smoothly, "Aren't you going to introduce us, Megan?" Then without waiting for a response, he held out his hand. "Hi, I'm Stephen Garrison."

Jade's father. Megan's former lover. The guy who just found out he has a child.

"I thought I recognized you!" Tiffany exclaimed. "You're the owner of the Garrison Grand, aren't you?"

"Yes," he acknowledged, then shook Tiffany's hand.

He was used to women stating the obvious when meeting him for the first time.

He knew his effect on the opposite sex. He was tall, well-built and rich. Three qualities women loved. When they weren't slipping him their phone numbers or hotel keys, they were finagling an introduction from friends.

His image blended with that of the Garrison Grand: life in the fast lane.

"Get around, don't you?" Megan remarked drily.

He arched a brow as he stepped toward where she stood, waiting for him. "I'm locally known, if that's what you mean."

He could tell Tiffany was following their exchange avidly, which made it all the more imperative that he and Megan find a place where they could speak privately.

"Listen to what Tiffany says, sweetheart," Megan said to her daughter before turning to walk toward the back door.

He followed, watching Megan's hips swing in tailored shorts and a light blue T-shirt, her feet in flip-flops.

She could have been any suburban mother trying to entertain her kid on a hot weekend afternoon.

Except now he knew she was the mother of *his* kid.

He trailed her through the house to a cozy living room furnished with tropical-print furniture and strewn with toys.

She stopped and turned to face him.

"Why the hell didn't you tell me I had a daughter?" he began without preamble. "And don't bother denying it. She's got the Garrison features, right down to the cleft chin!"

She folded her arms in front of her, almost hugging herself. "I thought it was best."

"You...thought...it...was...best?" Fury made him enunciate every word. "Best for whom? *You?* Because I can already tell you, honey, it sure as hell wasn't best for me." He stabbed his finger in the direction of the yard. "And it's questionable whether it was best for that little girl out there to be raised by you alone and denied all the advantages I could have provided for her."

He'd just given voice to her own niggling doubts over the years, Megan thought.

There were times when she'd thought about contacting Stephen. Times when she'd wondered whether she was doing the right thing by not telling him of Jade's existence.

And then she'd thought about his betrayal and his playboy lifestyle, and realized all over again he wasn't father material. There was no way he'd be happy to learn he'd accidentally fathered a child.

Now, though, he'd found out about Jade in the worst possible way.

Still, she rebelled at his judgment of her.

"Why?" he asked.

"It was clear to me our affair was coming to an end."

"Try again," he snapped. "You've used that line before. It may have sufficed as a reason for breaking up, but it doesn't explain why you kept my daughter from me."

"What would you have done if I'd told you?" she flung back at him. "Would you have accused me of deliberately getting pregnant? Of trying to trap you?"

He stared at her hard. "My reaction is beside the point. I had a right to know."

"You gave up that right when you proved yourself untrustworthy."

"Untrustworthy? What the hell is that supposed to mean?"

"It means you were seeing other women. *Having sex with other women.*"

He didn't move a muscle.

Just let him deny it, she thought angrily.

"You're crazy," he said finally.

"I saw *her,*" she responded, dropping her arms. "I saw her leaving your yacht the night I was coming—"

She cut herself off.

"The night you were coming to tell me you were pregnant?" he finished for her, guessing.

"She said you were the best she'd ever had."

"A nice compliment if it had been *true*," he retorted, "but I wasn't sleeping with anyone else."

She threw up her hands. "What was I supposed to think? She was straightening her dress while she spoke to me! She was leaving your yacht, it was late, and you had a reputation as a player."

A reputation that she'd been well aware of. She'd only gone out with him after he'd pursued her persistently while she'd worked on the renovation of Garrison headquarters. Even then, it had been against her better judgment. Of course, once she'd found out about his cheating, she'd castigated herself for her naiveté.

"I can hardly remember who you're talking about! Women have thrown themselves at me—"

"And that's the problem," she retorted. Definitely not Daddy material. Not then, and not now. "You're the Garrison Grand's owner. You operate in a sophisticated world."

A heartless world.

A muscle worked in his jaw. "Even if I'd slept with someone else, it doesn't justify your hiding Jade."

"Oh, yes, it does," she responded. "It meant as far as you were concerned, we weren't serious. It confirmed you were still a player. I knew you wouldn't be thrilled to discover I was pregnant."

If she couldn't trust him with her heart, how could she trust him with her baby?

At least, that's what she'd told herself whenever she'd had doubts about keeping Jade's existence a secret.

"How can you be so damn sure of my reaction when I'm not even sure what the hell my reaction would have been?" he tossed back, then raked his hand through his hair. "How could you have gotten pregnant? We used protection."

She'd wondered the same thing for a time. Now, she shrugged her shoulders. "I took some antibiotics for a sinus infection. They must have interfered with the pill."

He just continued to look at her fixedly.

She steadied herself. "The question is, where do we go from here?"

She dreaded raising the issue, but it was a question that had to be asked.

"I'll tell you where we're *not* going, and that's back to you excluding me from Jade's life."

His words chilled her. The thought of Jade somehow, someday, being taken away from her was her biggest fear.

"What do you mean?" she breathed.

"I mean," he said, his expression flinty, "you're going to marry me and publicly acknowledge I'm Jade's father."

"*What?* You can't be serious!" Even as her heart thudded, she tried to wrap her mind around the idea and couldn't.

"But I am, *sweetheart,*" he responded implacably.

"And if I say no?"

His face closed, hardening, and she got a glimpse of Stephen, the ruthless businessman. "Then I'll take you to court to establish my parental rights. I'll use every means at my disposal to give you the legal battle of your life and to get access to my daughter."

She knew those means were formidable. Stephen had wealth, power and political influence, not to mention the Garrison empire to back him up.

Still, she managed to find her voice, and say evenly, "I'd probably win a custody battle. The law is on my side as Jade's mother and the one who's raised her."

"You couldn't afford a fight, and even if you could, would you want to risk it?" he shot back.

No, she acknowledged, if only to herself. She knew Stephen had the money to hire the best lawyers in town, which would make for a protracted and messy battle. He could very well win generous visitation rights, at the least.

"Think about it," he said, seeming to read her mind. "One way or another, I'm in your life."

"I *could* fight you." She wasn't without some means herself. But she knew she was out of her league with Stephen.

And that was the heart of the matter. He'd always been out of her league, in every way.

"Yeah," he acknowledged too quietly, "but think about your career. You just got a new start in Miami. You don't have the time for a legal battle, and your professional reputation will take a hit."

She hated that he was right. Her professional reputation *would* suffer. Interior design was such a fickle business. Who would want to hire a woman whose personal life was a disaster? Who might be trailed by reporters to their doorstep?

Stephen had influence in this town. He was a trendsetter and more. She knew there would be people who'd want to keep on his good side—and that would include not doing business with the former lover with whom Stephen was involved in a messy child-custody fight.

"Why are you doing this me?" she whispered, distraught.

"Isn't that my line?" he countered. "Why did you do this to me?"

She opened and closed her mouth.

"No matter what," he said flatly, "we're joined at the hip."

"Oops, sorry to intrude!"

Megan turned and saw Tiffany standing in the doorway from the hallway to the living room. She had no idea how long the sitter had been there.

"I didn't realize you were still here, Megan," Tiffany said, "but I thought I'd check because you usually tell me when you're leaving." Then glancing from Stephen back to her, she added, "Didn't you say your dinner was at seven?"

Megan closed her eyes. She'd almost forgotten about her business dinner!

Opening her eyes again, she looked at her watch. It was nearing six. She'd have to hurry.

Tiffany looked from her to Stephen, and evidently judging that she'd walked in on a heated conversation, she took a step back. "I left Jade in the kitchen. Call me if you need anything."

When the sitter had retreated, Megan looked back at Stephen. "I have a business dinner in a little over an hour to court a potential new client. That's why Tiffany came over."

She'd made an exception to her rule not to let business intrude on her weekends with Jade because Conrad had asked her for a favor. She was supposed to meet Conrad and the potential client at a downtown Miami restaurant—and she wasn't even dressed yet.

Stephen looked at her coldly. "I'm giving you until Monday to make up your mind. And I'm only giving you that amount of time because I know you're scheduled to come by the Garrison Grand and we can talk then without having Jade around." He paused. "You already got *four* years."

Megan watched then as Stephen strode to the front door and slammed out of her house.

But *not* out of her life, she thought with a pang.

Five

The Mediterranean-style Garrison estate in Bal Harbour should have felt like home, but it didn't.

Still, Stephen reflected, even now with John Garrison gone, and his extramarital affair and its illegitimate child exposed, not to mention Bonita's heavy drinking, they all still felt obliged to maintain the illusion of a happy family gathering over Sunday dinner.

Yet, it was rare for all the Garrison siblings to be present, and tonight was no exception.

Stephen looked around the room. Bonita sat at the head of the dining room table, and his younger brother, Adam, and younger sister, Brooke, sat across from him.

Missing were Parker and Anna, and Brooke's twin, Brittany. Stephen figured the newlyweds had better things to do, lucky dogs. And since Brittany had recently decided she was in love with Emilio Jefferies, she preferred avoiding tense family dinners.

Now, as they chewed dinner mostly in silence, Stephen reflected on how an outsider might perceive tonight's gathering.

Valuable artwork hung on one wall, and in front of the opposite wall sat a china closet displaying various crystal pieces. Potted ferns sat in two corners of the room, and Greek columns flanked an arched entry. Overhead, a magnificent chandelier hung from a painted domed ceiling.

The room, like the rest of the estate, was majestic—and cold as ice.

His gaze came back to his family. Better to bite the bullet, he thought grimly.

"I just found out I have an illegitimate child," he announced into the silence.

Brooke gasped, and Adam froze.

Bonita stopped in midmotion, her wineglass halfway to her lips.

Given the shock waves that the discovery of John Garrison's illegitimate child had recently sent through the family, he had no illusions about how his news would be received.

Suddenly Bonita gave a raucous laugh. "Just

like your father, except you don't have a wife to trick."

He ignored the outburst, though it was uncharacteristic. He was the only one of the Garrison offspring that his mother didn't criticize, but he knew his news was a bombshell. "There's a three-year-old little girl named Jade."

"How?" Adam asked, raising the question he knew must be in everyone's mind.

He held his brother's gaze. "I had a relationship with her mother, Megan Simmons, when she did some interior design work at Garrison headquarters."

Bonita shook her head. "Just like your damned father!"

He heard the note of betrayal in his mother's tone, and felt his face tighten. "I'm planning on publicly acknowledging Jade as my daughter as soon as possible."

And marrying Megan, he added silently, if he got his way. He planned to do everything in his power to get his way.

Bonita's hand came down, her glass hitting the table with a thud and sending red wine across the white tablecloth. "You will do no such thing, do you hear me? I will not have the child of another tramp in this family! I will not tolerate another slut getting her hands on the Garrison fortune!"

He faced his mother. "You have no say in the matter," he ground out.

"I'm disappointed in you, Stephen," Bonita said, her voice frigid despite her inebriated state. "First your father betrays this family, then you do. Don't we have enough turmoil to deal with?"

In fact, he'd been thinking the same thing, but he rebelled at putting Megan in the same category as his father's faithlessness.

His fling with Megan may have been careless, but it sure as hell hadn't amounted to marital infidelity.

And it wasn't the fact that he had fathered a child out of wedlock that bothered him. It was having a child and not acknowledging her for years that, for him, created uncomfortable parallels with his father.

The longtime housekeeper, Lisette, appeared in the archway, no doubt having heard raised voices.

Bonita knocked a wine bottle to the floor, sending more wine, as well as glass this time, everywhere. Then she rose unsteadily to her feet.

Stephen stood, and Adam did the same.

Immediately, Lisette moved to Bonita's side. "Let me help you, Mrs. Garrison."

Stephen watched, along with Adam and Brooke, as Lisette helped Bonita from the room.

His hands bunched at his sides. He figured Lisette, as well as the missing Garrison family members, would find out soon enough what caused tonight's ruckus.

"Well, another rockin' Garrison family dinner!" Adam said, then picked up his glass and raised it in a mock salute before taking a swallow.

"Why don't we continue this conversation outside on the patio where the wet bar is?" he said to Adam and Brooke. Outside, they would be away from any prying eyes and open ears among the household staff. "We can let the staff clean up in here."

They'd almost finished with dinner, anyway. He looked down at the spilled wine and broken glass in distaste.

"Sorry," Brooke demurred. "I think I'll pass."

Stephen noticed his sister continued to look pale.

"Is something wrong?" he asked. "Did my news shock you that much?"

"N-no," she stammered.

He searched her face. "You look upset."

"I'm concerned about Mother's drinking." She lowered her voice. "Did you notice she drank almost a full bottle of wine at dinner—before she spilled the rest?"

Yeah, he had, and he hated to think how much his mother had imbibed *before* dinner.

Still, he had to admit that sometimes *he'd* felt the need for a fortifying drink before a Garrison family dinner.

They'd all moved to one end of the dining room, and he gently chucked Brooke under the chin. "Don't worry, kid. Let our mother deal with her own problems. But if it makes you feel better, I'm planning on having a talk with her."

Fat lot of good it would do, but he'd try. For some reason, today's dinner aside, Bonita usually held her tongue with him, and he figured that gave him some leverage. He'd also have to make clear that he wouldn't tolerate his mother taking any more cheap shots at Megan.

After he and Adam had said goodbye to Brooke and had retreated outdoors to the patio, he went to the marble-topped wet bar to pour himself a Scotch on the rocks.

The patio was dominated by an Olympic-size pool and lined with queen palms that swayed in the cool breeze. There was an unobstructed view of the ocean.

Their surroundings were serene, which made the recent tumult inside the mansion seem all the more out of place.

"Drink?" he asked Adam, who'd taken a seat on one of the bar stools.

"Booker's Bourbon, thanks."

From there, the conversation quickly moved to local business and politics. By an unspoken agreement, he and Adam put the ugly scene inside behind them as quickly as possible.

"The president of the Miami Business Council is

retiring next year," Stephen found himself observing after several minutes.

"Yeah, I know," Adam said. "I've been thinking of running to be his replacement."

Stephen shook his head. "The Business Council wants to uphold a certain image. Only married men have ever won election." He raised his glass and took a sip of his drink. "And you and I, little brother, are far from the image they want."

He and his brothers had well-earned reputations as players. Except now, Parker was married, and he'd probably be heading the same way soon, too, though he didn't feel the need to share that news with Adam just yet.

"So, what are you going to do about Jade? I'd like to meet her." Adam paused. "I'm an uncle, and I didn't even know it!"

"Try finding out that three years ago you became a father," Stephen replied ruefully. "And don't worry, you'll get to meet her."

All the Garrisons would, even if he had to move heaven and earth to make it happen.

His brows snapped together as he recalled Megan's accusation that he'd cheated. He could barely remember the night she'd referred to, or the woman who may or may not have tried to come on to him. But he knew he'd never two-timed anyone.

Still, he'd have to jog his memory somehow about

the night she was talking about. It infuriated him even now that she had continued to be skeptical even in the face of his denial.

"How *did* you feel when you found out you had a child?" Adam asked, curiosity lacing his words.

Stephen considered his brother's question. As he looked out at the water, Megan's words came back to him. *You wouldn't be thrilled to discover I was pregnant.*

Four years ago, he'd been happy to live in the moment. Yes, he'd given a passing thought to the fact that Megan was the one woman he could settle down with, but he hadn't taken any concrete steps in that direction. The truth was he'd have been blown away to discover he was a father.

Now, though, he thought about the little girl he'd seen yesterday. She looked like him, and he'd felt an instant connection.

He knew he wanted to be a father to Jade.

"It was unbelievable," he said, his gaze moving from the ocean to his brother. "She looks just like a Garrison, and the protectiveness automatically kicked in."

In fact, he was mad as hell at being shortchanged on the past three years.

"I've heard having a daughter changes everything for guys," Adam commented. "Suddenly you can't look at women the same way."

Tell me about it, Stephen thought, his mind traveling over all the women who'd blended into his past. Adam was right. He wouldn't want Jade to grow up and fall for the kind of smooth operator he'd been for most of his adult life.

"So, you're going to publicly acknowledge her?" Adam shook his head doubtfully. "I hope you know what you're getting into. As much as I hate echoing our mother, what do you know about Megan Simmons?"

"Enough," he said shortly.

"I remember meeting her when you dated four years ago," Adam went on. "Think she's one of those women who believes getting knocked up by a rich guy is like hitting the jackpot?"

"Shut up, Adam."

"No, really," his brother pressed.

"You don't know anything about it. She was hiding the kid's existence from me. I found out *accidentally* when I showed up at her house unannounced."

Adam whistled. "Well, that puts a different spin on things. I won't bother asking why you showed up at her house without an invitation." His brother gave him a sly look. "Still carrying a torch?"

"Shut up," he said, and downed some more of his drink.

It was late Sunday afternoon, and she and Anna Cross—no, Anna Garrison now, Megan corrected herself—sat at her dinette table enjoying some coffee and sinfully good Tres Leches cake.

Jade was playing in the living room, where they could hear and sometimes see her.

The house was big enough for Jade to play in, but small enough for just two people. Megan was glad now she'd taken up Anna's lease when she'd moved back to Miami. At the time, Anna had no longer needed the house in Coral Gables because she was marrying Parker Garrison.

Jade's uncle.

Of course, that meant Anna was Jade's aunt.

She really needed to 'fess up, Megan thought, looking at her friend.

She steeled herself and took a deep breath. "I have something to tell you."

"Mmm?" Anna responded, cutting off another piece of cake with her fork. "I shouldn't, but this is so—so yummy—"

"Jade is a Garrison."

Anna stilled for a moment, then her fork clattered against her plate. *"What?"*

Anna stared at her in disbelief, a dozen questions flitting across her face.

Megan rubbed clammy hands against her shorts. "Before you came to Miami four years ago, I dated Stephen Garrison."

"Stephen—?"

Megan nodded.

"I didn't even know the two of you had been involved!"

"It wasn't a long relationship." Though it had left its permanent mark. "It ended badly, and once it did, I was reluctant for a long time to share the details with anyone."

Now, though, she decided to fill in Anna on her past relationship and recent conversations with Stephen. Once she was done, she said, "He's threatened to go public. And he demanded I marry him."

"I can't believe you didn't tell him about Jade," Anna said. "Not that I'm passing judgment. It's just that I think I'd have found it hard to keep it secret."

And that was why, Megan thought, she hadn't confided in her closest friend about the details of Jade's paternity. She knew Anna would be working at Garrison, Inc. headquarters, and she didn't want to burden her friend with an explosive secret about the boss's brother.

Of course, she'd been tripped up by *not* having confided in Anna.

Anna looked thoughtful now that she seemed to have recovered from the initial shock. "I *knew* there was something between you and Stephen. I got some hints from Stephen's reaction when I mentioned you at dinner once. You also seemed to have a funny reaction at my wedding when he was heading our way."

"Actually, Stephen discovered I was back in Miami when you mentioned it to him," Megan said.

Anna's brow furrowed. "Oh, Megan, I'm *so* sorry! I didn't know how it would cause problems! All I wanted to do was send some business your way."

"Thanks." She reached out and patted Anna's hand soothingly. "I know you had the best intentions."

"And you know," Anna went on, "you *can* help Stephen. The Jefferieses are pressing *hard,* helped along by what Parker thinks is a corporate spy within the Garrison organization." Her lips twisted. "For a while, Parker—and, I guess, Stephen, as well— thought *I* was the spy."

"Yes, you explained it to me." She withdrew her hand and waved it around vaguely. "But now look at you. You're the glowing newlywed."

Anna laughed self-consciously, then murmured, "Parker…"

"*Believe me,* I'm very familiar with the charms of the Garrison men." Megan nodded her head toward the front room. "I have a daughter to prove it."

"But you don't regret Jade, do you?"

"No, of course not. She's wonderful. But now I have Stephen to deal with."

"All the Garrison men are alike," Anna observed obliquely. "What are you going to do?"

Megan sighed. "I'm not sure. Any suggestions?"

"Why don't you agree to marry him?"

"Are you serious? I can't!"

Obviously, Anna's eyes were clouded by love, Megan thought.

"Why not?"

Two simple words, and yet they dredged up a wealth of emotion, Megan thought. She was dangerously weak where Stephen was concerned, despite *everything*.

She'd seen that herself since he'd walked into her life again. It had been the same old feeling of excitement and overwhelming awareness—as if she couldn't stop arguing with him, and the only way to deal with it was to give in to the itch to jump his bones.

"He's a cheat," she contented herself with saying.

"Are you sure?" Anna pressed.

"You mean, am I sure I saw a woman with disheveled clothing emerging from Stephen's yacht, claiming to have seen more of him than his famous cleft chin?" Megan asked sarcastically. "Then, yes, I'm sure."

Anna cocked her head. "Well, even if he did cheat, that was four years ago. Now you have a child together. Think about Jade."

In fact, she had been thinking about Jade. Until now, Jade hadn't had a father in her life—though her own parents and family had been around in Indianapolis to shower her with love.

"You know," Anna went on, "being married to Stephen might not be so bad. It would take away some worries. Jade would grow up with everything money has to offer. You wouldn't have to worry about arriving at some complicated arrangement with Stephen for him to see her."

Yes, she thought, but she didn't know if *she* could take living under the same roof with Stephen. Sharing his bed…

Just being in the same room with him made her tense, jittery, and acutely aware of herself as a woman.

And she definitely couldn't risk her heart again. She'd cried for days, heartsick, when she'd discovered his betrayal four years ago.

At the time, she hadn't told him she was pregnant because she was sure a marriage between them would have been a disaster: he'd have cheated—he'd already proven himself capable of it—and she'd have wound up divorcing him to save herself.

There was *no way* she could marry him.

No way…no way…no way…

Unless…unless, of course, she could marry him without risking her heart again.

She paused.

Now, *there* might be a way out of her dilemma….

Six

Stephen stepped out of the elevators at Garrison, Inc., and the receptionist gave him a wide smile.

"Hi, Sheila."

"Hello, sugar." Sheila batted her eyelashes at him, and purred, "Come to make my day?"

He laughed. "I wish I could, honey, but duty calls."

Sheila pretended to pout.

The blue-eyed, blond, ex-Playboy bunny was his type, but this time, he knew his heart wasn't in their customary banter.

Damn Megan.

"Parker in his office?" he asked.

Sheila nodded.

"Thanks," he said, then walked down the hall.

He greeted Mario, who was pushing a mail cart and had been with the company since John Garrison's day, then a human resources person named Roberta, who was a recent hire.

All the while, he keenly observed every employee he passed. Someone in the firmament at Garrison, Inc. was passing along information to the Jefferies brothers, and until they discovered who it was, he and Parker and every other executive had to be careful about what they said and did within range of others.

Just last month, someone had accessed Parker's office computer and forwarded an e-mail they'd planted to Jordan Jefferies.

At his brother's partially closed office door, he rapped with his knuckles.

When he strode in, Parker said, "I hear congratulations are in order."

Closing the door, Stephen made for one of the leather chairs positioned before his brother's desk. "Thanks, but save it for after the wedding."

He was here because he and Parker had a Monday-morning appointment scheduled with Brandon Washington, the Garrison family lawyer. Brandon was always punctual, so Stephen knew he'd be here soon.

He caught his brother's raised eyebrows as he settled into his chair. "Somehow I knew the news would reach you one way or another."

Parker leaned back in his mesh swivel chair and tapped his fingertips together. "Maybe not the way you expected. Anna."

That caught his attention. "Anna?"

"I guess it's all right to disclose this now, since I also discovered you've been letting the news be known yourself." His brother paused. "Anna was over at Megan's place yesterday afternoon, and they had a little powwow."

Stephen felt his nostrils flare. "Tell me the wife encouraged Megan to do the sane thing."

Parker chuckled. "Define *sane*."

"Stuff it, Parker."

"Whoa, whoa, go easy here. I just discovered I'm an uncle."

Stephen let go with an expletive.

Parker eyed him. "You know, I should have known the minute I hired Megan four years ago that you'd find her irresistible. Of course, a redhead with flashing green eyes would send you down for the count."

"Yeah, well, I'm up again, and I intend to win this match. Why the hell didn't you tell me Anna and Megan were friends?"

His brother shrugged. "I had no idea myself until recently. It never came up. In fact, the first time I saw Megan again was at the wedding."

"You haven't reacted to my news with the same

suspicion it's been greeted with in other quarters," Stephen observed.

"Well, I *did* hire Megan, and I *am* married to Anna."

Just then a knock sounded, and both brothers turned to look at the door.

"Come in," Parker called.

Brandon walked in. "Good morning." He shut the door behind him. "I'm glad to see you're both here."

Stephen and Parker stood, and the men all shook hands.

Brandon took the other chair facing Parker.

"So what do we have, Brandon?" Stephen asked, as he and Parker sat back down.

"Cassie Garrison is still refusing to deal," Brandon stated matter-of-factly.

Stephen suppressed a snort of disgust.

At the reading of his father's will two months ago, he, along with the rest of the family, had discovered John Garrison had fathered a daughter during an extramarital affair with Ava Sinclair, a local he'd met in the Bahamas.

On top of it all, it turned out that the daughter was Cassie Sinclair, the manager of the Garrison Grand-Bahamas hotel, and that she, along with the five legitimate Garrison siblings, had inherited shares in the family business.

Stephen's lips twisted. Cassie Sinclair now chose to go by the name Cassie Sinclair Garrison.

Something had to be done.

So far, Cassie had resisted Parker's overtures and refused to turn over her shares in the Garrison empire.

"She apparently just wants to be left alone to run the Garrison Grand-Bahamas," Brandon said.

"No dice," Parker responded.

Brandon sighed. "I'm not getting anywhere by phone. Frankly, our best option is if I go down there and try to negotiate in person for a deal to buy her out."

Parker laced his fingers together. "I have no problem with that plan." Parker glanced over at Stephen for his assent before looking back at Brandon. "We're willing to pay—within reason."

Brandon named what he'd offered as a reasonable price for Cassie's shares, and Stephen's hand flexed on his armrest.

"You lowballed her first?" Stephen heard himself ask.

"Of course," Brandon said.

Stephen trusted Brandon like a brother. The Washingtons—Brandon and his father before him—had been the family legal advisors for years. Still, it was vitally important they get this problem with Cassie wrapped up soon and to their satisfaction. They couldn't let the future of the Garrison empire rest with an unknown quantity—a potential loose cannon.

"And if she still refuses to sell after I approach her in person?" Brandon asked, voicing the question on all their minds.

"Everyone has their price," Parker said grimly. "We'll have to think about how much more we're willing to offer."

Stephen arched a brow. "Or we can borrow a page from the world of celebrity." He looked over at Brandon. "When you get down there, why don't you first see if you can dig up some dirt on Cassie's past? It'll give us some leverage to force her hand."

Parker nodded thoughtfully. "With stakes like this, I'll take any ammunition I can get."

When Megan walked into Stephen's office at Garrison, Inc., she had some design plans in hand. But more importantly, she had a decision.

Stephen stepped around his desk and strode toward her.

"I've drawn up some preliminary plans," she said. "You can take a look at them at your leisure, and then we can discuss them. Anything can be changed, of course."

He took the plans from her and dropped them on a nearby table. Then he shut his office door and braced his arm there. "Well?"

They both knew the real topic of this meeting.

She told herself she wasn't afraid of him. She

wasn't afraid of the vast Garrison family wealth and influence. But she had to face reality.

She chewed her lip. "I've thought about your proposal."

His *proposal* had been a far cry from her girlhood dreams, but those she'd buried along with their relationship four years ago.

"Good. I expected you to."

She walked farther into the room, and he followed.

Stephen's immense office had a view of the beach and endless blue water. His desk stood in front of floor-to-ceiling windows, and off to one side were a sofa and chairs arranged around a low table.

Like the rest of the hotel, the office was light and airy. The only thing she'd change was the abstract artwork. Though she was sure it was all very valuable, she'd prefer to see something less geometrical and more soft, maybe impressionist.

But more importantly, the view from Stephen's windows said everything, and *that* she couldn't change. She watched as a toned blonde walked past to head into the hotel.

She turned toward Stephen.

His too-handsome face gave nothing away.

Nervous energy thrummed through her. She rubbed a palm against her taupe linen skirt. "I've decided to accept your proposal."

His eyes shot dark fire, and she could read the

triumph in them. "We'll have the wedding next weekend."

Her stomach flipped over. "*Next weekend?* That's not enough time!"

She'd thought she'd have more time to adjust to the idea of being Mrs. Stephen Garrison.

"You've already had four years," he said in a clipped voice, as if he'd read her mind.

"A week is not enough time to plan a wedding—"

A grim smile slashed his face. "It is if we have it here at the Garrison Grand, where *conveniently* I'm the boss. In fact, I just put together Parker and Anna's wedding in a short time."

"I have a job I just started," she began.

"You won't need to do anything but show up."

She stared at him doubtfully.

"Let's seal the deal." He looked at her innocently. "I hope that's okay?"

Then before she could react, he pulled her into his arms, and his lips came down on hers.

First there was the warm pressure of his mouth, then he slipped inside, his tongue touching and coaxing hers.

Hot, sweet sensation flooded her, and a rainbow of colors danced behind her eyelids.

When he eventually pulled back, he gave her a heavy-lidded look. "Just like I remembered," he murmured.

She touched her fingertips to her lips, feeling him there still.

Ordinarily, the stolen kiss might have sparked her ire, but under the circumstances, it reminded her of what she had to do.

She dropped her hand. "I forgot to mention something," she said hoarsely.

"What's that?"

She took a breath. "I have a couple of conditions of my own."

His look turned guarded. "Shoot."

"I want to wait until after the wedding to explain to Jade that you're her biological father."

He looked ready to argue, so she rushed on. "I want to give her time to adjust. It's enough for the moment that I'm springing this wedding on her."

"Aren't you just drawing this out when it would be better to explain the whole thing at once?"

She shook her head. "I want her to get used to you…get to know and—and like you, first, without putting any sense of obligation on her three-year-old shoulders."

"Fine," he said, though she knew he still wasn't thrilled with her idea.

And now for the hard part, she thought.

"I'm agreeing to this marriage for Jade's sake," she said. "I know there'll be lots of advantages to growing up a Garrison and with you there to help raise her."

He nodded, as if he was glad she saw reason.

"That's why," she went on, her chin coming up, "this will be a marriage in name only. I'm doing this for Jade. I won't sleep with you, Stephen."

Something in his eyes flared, and his lips curled. "Strong words from a woman who just melted into my kiss."

"Those are my conditions," she repeated.

Their eyes held for one drawn-out moment.

"You'll get your own bedroom," he said finally.

She relaxed. She was thankful for the walls of a bedroom. Now she just had to work on shoring up the ones around her heart.

When she pushed back the tissue paper, Megan felt the breath leave her.

A short while ago, a messenger had delivered several boxes. She'd taken the delivery, puzzled but knowing from the sender's information that it came from Stephen. She'd wondered why he hadn't bothered to bring the boxes himself, since he was due to arrive in a short time.

Now, Megan let her fingers stroke over the smooth white satin revealed when she'd opened the first box.

A multitude of conflicting emotions stormed her.

She understood now why Stephen may have chosen to send the boxes by messenger before he arrived. Once she'd seen what he'd bought for her, he'd known she'd find it hard to resist.

Carefully, she lifted the gown from the box and examined it.

It was a backless sheath dress with a small swallowtail train made of satin overlaid with lace. The bodice, which had a sweetheart neckline, was held up by two spaghetti straps.

Simple but sexy, it would be spectacular with her flaming red hair, as well as show off her generous chest to advantage.

Stephen knew her so well. And *that,* she realized, was part of the problem.

She'd told Stephen she'd be wearing something practical—something she already owned—for the wedding. Instead, he'd overridden her.

He'd sent her this dress, and its message was clear: she was being served up as a delicious dessert he intended to savor.

Still, the dress was so beautiful, it brought tears to her eyes.

She'd once wished for happily-ever-after. Instead, she was getting an illusion.

A sham wedding leading to a fake marriage.

Tamping down a sudden well of emotion, she forced herself to open the rest of the boxes.

One box contained a pair of stylish stiletto sandals. Another held an adorable sleeveless flower girl's dress with a high ribbon waist and matching white sandals.

Her heart squeezed as she thought of Jade and how delighted she'd be.

When she opened the last box, however, her reaction changed, and she felt heat course through her.

The box contained a white bustier, matching lacy underwear and thigh-high hosiery.

Unbidden, images of modeling the sexy concoction for Stephen went through her mind.

Then, annoyed with herself, she let her hand drop away from the box.

Of course, Stephen had no trouble picking out her size. He was a connoisseur of the female form, she reminded herself. A playboy extraordinaire.

She was torn from her thoughts by the sound of the doorbell.

Moments later, she heard the sound of running feet.

"Mommy, there's someone at the door!" Jade called out.

"I'll be right there."

She and Stephen had agreed he'd come over on Wednesday night in order to ease the transition for Jade to the upcoming marriage.

She'd already explained to Jade as well as she could that she'd be getting married to Stephen and they'd be known as Megan and Jade Garrison.

Now, she prayed Stephen's get-to-know-you session with his daughter went well.

When she opened the door, with Jade peering around her, she was presented with an incongruous sight. Stephen held a bouquet of flowers in one hand, and a large brown-haired, brown-eyed baby doll in the other.

As annoyed as she'd just been with him, she couldn't help reacting with a laughing gasp.

His eyes met hers, and she saw laughter lurking within them. "She rode in the front passenger seat."

Wide-eyed, Jade stared at Stephen.

Megan covered her mouth.

Not a word, Stephen's eyes mockingly warned her. Then he stepped forward. "Hello, honey."

Megan stared at him—dressed as the consummate corporate executive in a charcoal business suit—before he bent forward and kissed her on the lips.

"We need to make this good for Jade," he murmured as he straightened.

She gave him a startled look, then closed the door behind him. What was he up to?

But Stephen was already looking down at his daughter. He smiled. "Hello, Jade."

Jade edged closer to her, and Megan put a comforting arm behind her.

"Hi," Jade said hesitantly.

Megan realized with a start that Jade was uncharacteristically shy. Apparently, it was one thing to enthusiastically point out a stranger—as Jade had done when Stephen had appeared in their backyard on Saturday—and another to welcome someone more permanent.

Megan prayed again or all their sakes that tonight went well.

Stephen held out the baby doll, which was dressed in pink and purple and wore a headband. "I have a present for you. This is Abby, and she's looking for a home."

Jade eyed the doll, then looked back at Stephen.

Megan saw a flicker of uncertainty in Stephen's eyes, and her heart went out to him. He was clearly lost.

"Stephen bought a gift for you, isn't that nice?" she said to Jade.

They'd agreed Jade would call him Stephen until she got used to him in her life.

Jade stepped forward, then took the doll and hugged it to her. "Thank you."

Megan watched as Stephen's eyes went to her again. "And these are for you."

The bouquet that he held out to her contained lilies mixed with lavender. Her favorite. He'd sent the flowers to her when they'd dated, and he'd remembered still.

"Thank you."

Their hands brushed over the flowers, and a sizzle

went through her. And though her mind flashed danger, her heart beat rapidly.

She steadied herself. "Why don't we go into the living room? Dinner is almost ready. Would you like anything to drink, Stephen?"

"A beer would be great."

Jade was already playing with her doll, and Stephen planted himself halfway between the kitchen and where the little girl sat.

Megan felt a small smile rise to her lips. Big, bad Stephen Garrison was in unfamiliar territory, rendered helpless by a three-year-old.

She could see the headline: Playboy Beaten by Child's Play.

When she came out with Stephen's beer, she noticed Jade looking at him from the corner of her eyes.

The little girl stood, then blurted, "Would you like to see my toys?"

She watched the play of emotions on Stephen's face, before he responded casually, "Sure. Let's see what you got, kid."

Her heart constricted as she watched Stephen follow Jade, and a variety of emotions swept over her.

Finally, she headed back to the kitchen. She had chicken Kiev in the oven and potatoes and broccoli on the stove.

Dinner would be a far cry from what Stephen was used to at Miami's top-tier restaurants, including the ones within the Garrison Grand itself. She had to give a nod to kid fare, but she reminded herself that Stephen was better off finding out sooner rather than later what parenthood was about. He was determined to come into her life and Jade's, and she wasn't going to sugarcoat it for him.

When she'd gotten everything on the table, she went to find them—the most important person in her life, and the one around whom her world had revolved four years ago.

She located them in Jade's room.

"…and this is Holly, and that's Caroline," her daughter said.

Megan watched as Stephen nodded. "Quite a crowd."

Jade had all her dolls and stuffed animals lined up, and apparently had been introducing them all to Stephen.

"Dinner's ready," Megan heard herself say.

Stephen and Jade both turned to her.

"But, Mommy, I still need to introduce my dolls!"

"Later, sweetie."

Stephen winked. "I promise I'll come back after dinner, pumpkin."

Jade pulled a face but trudged in the direction of the kitchen.

Pumpkin?

It was a big turnaround from where Stephen and

Jade had been a mere thirty minutes ago, and Megan was reminded again of the fact that a three-year-old's worldview could do a one-eighty in a minute.

She watched Jade leave, then looked back at Stephen. "Quick work there."

He gave her a lazy smile. "Charm upsets you?"

She forced herself to shrug indifferently. "Your *legendary* charm. Why should I be surprised?"

"Afraid you'll fall under it again?" he challenged.

"I've been inoculated for life."

He chuckled as he sauntered toward her. "Don't worry. I leave my best for someone…special."

She sucked in a breath, but he didn't try to steal a kiss or make a pass.

Instead, he walked out of the room and followed Jade's lead.

She expelled the breath she was holding, then followed him out.

In the house's little dining area, she saw Stephen eyeing the floral display in the center of the table.

She'd set his bouquet there in a clear glass vase.

"Very nice," he commented, "if I do say so myself."

"I put them there so we wouldn't have to stare at each other across the table through dinner," she muttered in a low voice as she went past.

He had the audacity to laugh, which just sent a shiver through her because she remembered how much she'd always liked his laugh.

She felt his arm snake around her, and he gave her a quick kiss on the neck. "Glad you like them so much."

"You know flowers that stand for *devotion* are my favorite," she retorted.

At dinner, Jade kept up a steady stream of conversation with Stephen. She seemed openly curious about him now.

He handled her questions well, simplifying but never talking down to her, and it was clear that though he was still feeling his way, he was gaining confidence with every passing second.

Megan watched the interaction and thought they could all be any family having dinner together. Except this was a pretend family with an upcoming sham marriage.

Seven

So far, Stephen thought, things were working out as he'd planned.

Jade was warming to him, and while he had further to go with Megan, he knew at least that she was far from being immune to him.

"Want to see the rest of my dolls?" Jade piped up as soon as dinner was over.

"Sure."

Jade's face lit up. She ran around the table to grab his hand and tug him forward as he stood.

"Jade, we don't drag guests around like toys," Megan warned. "Stephen isn't Barney."

"Yes, Mommy," Jade responded without looking at her mother.

Stephen felt a smile pull at his lips.

She reminded him of himself when he was a little kid—full of boundless energy and enthusiasm. He wondered which parts of herself Megan saw in Jade.

It was still hitting him that this little girl was *his*. He wouldn't—couldn't—let her down.

Twenty minutes later, Jade was instructing him on tea party etiquette using her table-and-chair set and toy kitchen when Megan appeared in the doorway.

His eyes ate her up. He'd discarded his jacket and tie before dinner, but she was dressed even more casually in a flower-print short-sleeved blouse, tailored beige cropped pants and espadrille sandals.

Memories tugged and he remembered the way they used to dance together at some of Miami's hottest nightspots.

Their bodies had brushed, swayed and come together again. They'd tantalized each other before heading home to make passionate love on silk sheets.

Realizing he'd been staring at Megan and she'd begun looking back at him questioningly, he suddenly felt ridiculous.

It was absurd to be having sexy thoughts about Megan while he was sitting in a girly pink bedroom, waiting to drink pretend tea from a toy cup.

Covering his lapse, he said, "Have you shown Jade her flower girl dress?"

Megan hesitated, but Jade perked up, "Dress? What color?"

"Pink, of course," he informed her.

Jade squealed and clapped her hands. "Can I see? Can I see?"

Megan sighed. "It's on my bed, Jade."

Stephen noted Megan didn't seem too happy with his gift. He was doubly glad now he'd let the cat out of the bag and gotten the jump on her.

They followed Jade to Megan's bedroom, which was decorated in tropical colors of lime-green, peach and pink. White wicker furniture blended with a couple of antique pieces.

His eyes fell to the bed, where some of his purchases from yesterday lay in and out of their boxes. The lingerie he'd sent was nowhere to be seen but a tulle-and-satin flower girl dress with a wide sash and little rosebud embroidery along the neckline lay spread out across the bed.

Jade oohed and aahed over the dress before announcing, "I love it!"

"I wasn't sure of the size, so I had to guess."

"It's her size," Megan said gloomily from next to him.

He tossed her an amused look, and she raised an

eyebrow at him. Clearly there'd be a battle later, but he was more than up for it.

After Megan gave in to Jade's pleas to try on the dress, and the little girl had twirled around for them, Megan announced it was time for dessert.

They all went back to the dining room to have what Stephen discovered was Jade's favorite: mint chocolate chip ice cream with chocolate syrup.

Afterward, the three of them cleared the table and Megan said it was Jade's bedtime.

Jade put up some resistance, but gave up the fight when Stephen agreed to read a bedtime story.

Only after he'd read three of Jade's favorite stories were he and Megan able to head back to the living room.

Once there, Megan folded her arms. "I can't accept the gifts you sent."

"Then I suppose you're really not going to like this." He reached into his pocket, then picked up her hand and slid a ring onto her finger.

He heard her breath catch, hitch.

Yesterday, he'd gone to one of Miami's most exclusive jewelers and bought an engagement ring with a large Canadian diamond in the center flanked by two emeralds.

"The stones signify our yesterday, today and tomorrow," he told her. "I chose emeralds for your eyes."

"We're not having much of an engagement," she said, staring at the ring.

"We're just condensing the steps."

She looked up at him, then started to pull the ring off, but he stopped her.

Her chin came up. "Do you want a symbolic reminder of our yesterdays, Stephen?"

His mouth tightened. "Do you regret having Jade?"

"You know that's not what I meant!"

"Then what did you mean?" he challenged her. "Do I want to remember nights of mind-blowing sex? Do I want to remember the way we were so hot for each other, we couldn't be in the same room without getting turned on?"

Their eyes locked.

He'd opened the door, and their past came flooding back. One touch, one kiss, right now, and Stephen knew they'd both be swept away.

"I was waiting to discuss the packages with you, but now that you made her aware of the dress, Jade is all excited."

"Yeah, well, consider yourself outmaneuvered."

The air between them shimmered with sexual energy.

"And what about that kiss when you first walked in?"

He gave her a rakish smile. "What about it?"

"What did you mean by 'we need to make this good for Jade'?"

He sobered. "I mean, if this marriage is about doing what's best for Jade, then we need to make her believe we're happily married."

She stalked away, then whirled back. "You're just using Jade as an excuse."

Busted. "For what?" he asked innocently.

"You know what. To put the moves on me, hoping to get me back in bed."

"When we wind up back in bed, it'll be because you'll want it as badly as I do."

"You're not even going to try to deny it, are you?"

"In fact—" he glanced back toward Jade's room "—since Jade's asleep now, I'm going to suggest we practice." He took a step toward her.

Her eyes widened. "Definitely not necessary," she said sharply.

"But oh so enjoyable. Did you like the lingerie I sent?"

She flushed. "Strumpet & Pink. You *do* know your lingerie, and why am I not surprised?"

He was close enough now to see the pulse jump at the side of her throat.

He smoothed a lock of her hair with the back of his hand, and her eyes sparked before his gaze dropped to her mouth.

He'd always liked her fire. As much as he liked

her mouth, in fact. It was full and made for kissing. He remembered all she'd done with that mouth, and nearly groaned aloud.

"You had an amazing collection," he muttered against her lips, "and a fabulous body to go with it."

Then he kissed her, sinking into her with a hunger that surprised even him. There was a moment when she didn't react, but then her mouth opened to him.

He deepened the kiss and brought his hand up to cup her breast, feeling the nipple harden through the thin fabric of her bra and top.

Lust slammed into him, and just like that he was aroused.

She'd always been able to turn him on faster than any woman ever had, and apparently nothing much had changed.

He had to have her. In bed and out. He *would* have her.

It gave him some satisfaction to be in control—to be calling the shots. It was what he was used to.

But if he didn't stop this make-out session soon, he was in danger of losing it. Tonight wasn't the night for seduction—just for giving her a taste.

Jade was sleeping nearby, and he didn't want to scare Megan off a wedding when he almost had her where he wanted her.

He eased back from their kiss. When he raised his head, he met her lambent gaze.

"Was that kiss supposed to prove something to me?" she asked.

"Yeah. We won't have any problems convincing Jade." Hell, his body still raged for her, and it was only with effort he got it under control.

Her brows drew together. "Of course not. You're a playboy of mythical proportions."

He refrained from gibing about what proportions she was talking about. Instead, he said, "I won't cheat because my father was a cheater."

That got her attention.

"What?" She stopped, and her brow puckered again. "What do you mean?"

"I mean, my father had an extramarital affair, and we only found out about his twenty-seven-year-old love child at the reading of his will recently. Suffice it to say, the news wreaked havoc on the family, particularly my mother."

He filled her in on his family's discovery of the existence of Cassie Sinclair Garrison and her claim on the Garrison fortune.

"You do have problems, don't you?" she said. "The Jefferieses on one hand, and now your father's illegitimate child."

"Don't forget *my* illegitimate child, but I'm about to fix that situation."

Megan folded her arms. "So I'm supposed to conclude from the Cassie story that you've reformed?"

Her coolness and continued skepticism ate at him. He picked up his jacket from where he'd thrown it on the back of a chair at the beginning of the evening. "You're supposed to conclude we'll have a *real* marriage."

He gave her a lingering look—sparks shooting back and forth between them—before he let himself out of the house.

The wedding ceremony was held on a private slice of beach behind the Garrison Grand, where Parker and Anna's wedding had taken place the month before.

A floor had been laid over the sand, and folding chairs had been set up on either side of a makeshift aisle. Off to the side, adjacent to the hotel, was a canopied area that would serve as the location for an indoor-outdoor reception.

Because of the short notice, and the small number of guests, the local media had not caught wind of the pending nuptials.

Now, as Megan stood behind Jade and next to her father in the shade of the hotel's lobby, waiting for the string quartet to strike up Pachelbel's *Canon,* she was profoundly grateful for the relative privacy.

She was nervous enough as it was.

This week, she'd had to break the news to both her family and her employer that she was about to have a hasty wedding to Stephen Garrison.

Her parents and younger sister had known at least that Stephen was the father of her child, though they'd kept a vow of secrecy for the past four years.

She'd simply told them that she and Stephen had reconnected when she'd moved back to Miami and that the two of them had realized they were destined to be together.

Her mother had nonetheless worried about whether Megan was making the right decision, but Megan had kept a determined, upbeat front. Her entire immediate family had decided to fly down to Miami for the weekend for the ceremony.

Breaking the news to her coworkers at Elkind, Ross had been a trickier matter. They'd been surprised and even astonished to discover she and Stephen were going to marry. None of them had even been aware that she and Stephen had been involved in the past, because she'd been discreet about her affair with the middle Garrison brother four years before.

She'd had to explain that she and Stephen had reconnected over her work on the Garrison Grand and known immediately they'd made a mistake by parting ways.

Once she'd assured everyone that Elkind, Ross would continue to have the Garrison account, and she'd continue to work on it with the utmost professionalism, everyone's initial curiosity at least had been satisfied. Conrad Elkind was even attending the ceremony today along with his wife.

By far the hardest disclosure for her to deal with had been the announcement to the media. She'd helped Stephen draft a public statement that would be released right after the wedding. She'd combed over every word of the announcement of her marriage and the disclosure that Jade was Stephen's child.

She was suddenly recalled from her reverie as the instrumentalists struck up Pachelbel's *Canon*.

The assembled guests turned to look at her, and she in return surveyed them. Even Bonita Garrison was in attendance, though Stephen had warned her that his mother had drawn unpleasant comparisons between their situation and the hurt caused by her late husband's philandering.

Her eyes drifted to Stephen, and she only had eyes for him as she started down the aisle created by the partitioned guests.

His expression was carved in granite—except for his eyes. As she drew closer, she saw that his eyes shone with sensuous promise.

She had to remind herself it was a well-practiced look for him and she shouldn't attach too much significance to it.

Still, when she reached his side, and they turned to face the officiant, tears pricked her eyes and she trembled.

There were times when she'd wished Jade had had a father around, and now Stephen had stepped up to the plate—whether she wanted him to or not.

She handed her round bouquet of tightly packed roses to Jade.

"We have been called here today to witness Megan and Stephen being joined together in holy matrimony…"

As the officiant went on, she was very aware of Stephen standing by her side and she stole a look at him. He was steady as a rock, facing forward, his expression serious.

Maybe because he felt her observation, however, he turned his head and glanced down at her.

She blinked rapidly to clear the mist from her eyes.

"Who gives this woman to be wedded to this man?"

"I do!" Jade piped up, and the guests laughed.

She and Stephen laughed, too, and then her breath caught. She hadn't seen Stephen laugh like that in four years.

And all at once, it was time to say her vows.

"I, Megan, take you, Stephen, to be my husband…" Her voice came out a little unsteady, but Stephen held her gaze, refusing to let her look away.

When it was his turn, he looked into her eyes and spoke in a sure and clear voice. "I, Stephen, take you, Megan, to be my wife…"

His words gave her goose bumps, and the goose

bumps turned to a fine tremor when it was time to exchange rings.

She wondered if Stephen could feel her unsteadiness as he took her hand and slipped a filigreed platinum band next to her engagement ring.

"Take this ring as an eternal symbol of my love…"

She couldn't look away from him as he said the words and then it was her turn to repeat them back to him.

"…I now pronounce you…"

Married. The word echoed in her head, and she felt the full effect of its heady power.

Stephen had changed the course of her life already, and now he was her husband.

Her husband, and he was bending forward, a dark glimmer in his eyes and lust in his soul.

"Let's make it good for Jade," he murmured.

His lips touched hers, and before she could react, he'd deepened the kiss to a long and lingering one she felt down to the toes. Her hands curled into his upper arms.

The guests hooted and clapped.

Stephen straightened, and she took a deep breath. Then she hooked her arm through his and they walked past their guests and toward the hotel to the tune of "Ode to Joy."

Fortunately, once the reception started under tents set up on the beach, she was able to mingle among

the guests and push aside—at least for the moment—
the disturbing feelings Stephen aroused in her.

As she watched Jade dance with Stephen, Anna
come over to congratulate her.

Her friend gave her a quick hug. "I'm so glad you
married into the family, even if I have selfish reasons.
The Garrisons *can* be intimidating."

"Tell me about it," Megan muttered. She'd met all
of the Garrison siblings when she and Stephen had
dated, so she had an inkling. Then she thought about
how hard a time she had handling just Stephen.

Anna searched her face. "So are you satisfied with
your decision?"

"Thanks for dispensing with the word *happy,*" she
responded. They both knew this forced marriage was
anything but a joyous occasion.

"You should give Stephen a chance. He might
surprise you."

"It'll be difficult to surprise me. This time I won't
be shocked if I find another woman in his bed."

Stephen was still dancing with Jade, who was
twirling around. It wasn't hard to see how they were
related—the dark-haired little girl who was smiling
and laughing, and the darkly gorgeous father who
somehow managed to look comfortable dancing with
an unpredictable partner.

"You shouldn't be such a cynic," Anna admonished.

Megan looked back at her. "It's precisely because

I don't think he can be faithful that I made sure this would be a marriage in name only."

"What do you mean?"

"I mean—and this is confidential—we won't be sleeping together."

Anna's eyebrows shot up. "Stephen agreed?"

She recalled Stephen's challenges, then his gambit regarding making things look good for Jade. "He agreed to separate bedrooms."

Anna looked at her shrewdly. "Uh-huh."

Megan glanced over at the man who'd sent her life careening off course ever since he'd stepped into it four years ago. "I won't lose my heart to him again," she said adamantly.

Eight

He was, Stephen decided, a masochist.

Looking at Megan in the wedding gown *he'd* picked out, all he wanted to do was spirit her away to a place where they could get naked and find feverish deliverance.

His yacht would serve the purpose well. He kept it nearby, and it was somewhere he could relax and get away from it all. Its satin-covered bed was his favorite place to make love, rocked by the soothing waves lapping the sides of the boat.

His body had been at a steady hum ever since he'd seen Megan start down the aisle. He hadn't been able to peel his eyes off her. She'd looked incredible in the simple but sexy gown he'd picked up for her at a high-end Miami boutique.

He was getting what he wanted, but he wanted her *willing*. Despite her attempt to make this a marriage of convenience, he planned to seduce her back into his bed—as the first step toward making them the family unit they should be.

He'd seen tears in her eyes during the ceremony, and had wondered whether they signaled sadness or happiness. When she was in his arms, he'd make sure she was beyond sadness or happiness. They'd just *fit,* as they had from the very beginning.

He absently twisted the ring on his finger.

"Still getting used to the feel? Don't worry, you will, faster than you can believe."

He turned at the sound of his brother's voice. "Hey, Parker."

"What are you thinking?"

"Nothing."

"*Nothing* is a lot when you're the groom, and it's your day," his brother commented.

Stephen watched Megan float among the guests. She stopped to speak with Conrad and his wife and accept congratulations.

"Be careful," Parker murmured, following the direction of his gaze. "At this rate, you'll be falling for her all over again, and she'll have you eating out of the palm of her hand."

"Not gonna happen."

He wanted Megan, but he was done with surprises coming out of left field. This time he was in control.

He scanned the guests, then gave his brother a lopsided smile. "I pulled this thing together in a week. I'm getting good at it. Think any of our other siblings wants a spur-of-the-moment wedding?"

Parker groaned. "Don't even think it. It's bad enough Brittany thinks she's getting hitched to a Jefferies."

"Speaking of which," Stephen responded, spying Brittany and her fiancé, Emilio Jefferies, "looks like some guests are heading our way."

"Yeah, *Jefferies,*" Adam grated as he joined them from where he'd been standing a few feet away.

Parker turned in the direction of their gaze, and watched, too, as their younger sister approached with the darker of the Jefferies brothers.

Stephen had gotten a chance to size the man up when Emilio had crashed Parker and Anna's wedding. Unlike his brother, Emilio was dark haired and olive skinned, his green eyes a startling contrast to his complexion.

From an investigative report that Parker had ordered, Stephen knew Emilio had been adopted. His mother had been the Jefferies' nanny, and he'd been born in Cuba.

"Hola," Brittany said, smiling as she came toward them holding Emilio's hand.

Emilio, in contrast, looked as guarded as he and his brothers probably did, Stephen noted.

"We just wanted to say congratulations, Stephen." She stepped forward and brushed his cheek with a quick kiss.

"Thanks, kiddo." Then he looked up, and said in acknowledgment, "Jefferies."

Emilio held out his hand. "Congratulations."

It was a bold move, and after a split second, he reached out to grasp Emilio's hand. "Thanks."

He and his brothers had their suspicions, but while signs pointed to corporate espionage by the Jefferieses, they'd yet to uncover the trail and, more importantly, find the culprit.

In the meantime, it was clear Emilio was devoted to Brittany, and Stephen figured that had to count for something—at least for a cool but civilized exchange of pleasantries at a wedding. And, if there was one thing he'd learned in the corporate world, it was never to let the competition see you sweat.

Parker looked narrow-eyed. "Good to see you, Jefferies."

Adam nodded his head in acknowledgment.

Brittany beamed, and Parker caught the look.

"It's easy to be charitable when this is one wedding Emilio isn't crashing," Parker said to his sister wryly.

Adam coughed to hide a laugh, and, if he wasn't

mistaken, Stephen thought, a glint of humor appeared in Emilio Jefferies's eyes.

As he turned to say something more to Brittany, however, he spotted one of his hotel employees wheeling in the table with the wedding cake.

He grasped his brothers' arms, and nodded at his sister and Emilio. "You'll excuse me. Business—of the pleasant variety—calls."

She'd visited Stephen's private estate near South Beach four years ago, but this time around it was home—and Megan found herself adjusting to the idea.

She and Stephen had agreed she'd give up the lease on the cute little house in Coral Gables and move into his four-bedroom Spanish Mission-style home. She knew the grounds of the estate included a pool, while the house itself had a gym and a home theater.

Even a little girl as active and rambunctious as Jade would have a hard time making a dent in such a place.

Megan consoled herself with that thought now, as she prepared to get out of her wedding gown and get ready for bed in the bedroom next to Stephen's.

Her room and Stephen's were separated only by a connecting bathroom, and Stephen had explained that while his bedroom was the master suite, hers had been set up as a baby's room by the house's previous owners. Since Jade was occupying the third bedroom, which was ideally configured for use as a child's room, and the fourth was being used by Stephen as a guest bedroom/upstairs office, there was no place else for her to stay.

She sighed now as she looked around the room, toying with the bouquet she'd held earlier in the day as she'd walked down the aisle.

The room was outfitted with Spanish colonial-style furniture, in keeping with the house's architecture. Rich, sturdy wood furniture contrasted with white walls and wrought-iron accent pieces.

Four years ago, when she'd spent nights at Stephen's estate, she'd imagined this room one day being used as a nursery for their child. Now Jade was already past the need for a nursery, and she and Stephen wouldn't have any more children.

The thought inexplicably depressed her, just as the entire day had been an emotional maelstrom for her.

After the wedding reception, she and Stephen had headed back to his estate and put a very tired Jade to bed. Jade had promptly fallen asleep in her new bedroom, down the hall from hers and Stephen's.

There hadn't been time to move all their possessions from the Coral Gables house to Stephen's place before the wedding, but since she'd already paid the current month's rent, she knew she had some time to move out, though she'd given notice she'd be giving up the lease.

With any luck, Jade would settle right into their

new routine. She'd still drop Jade off at preschool, and Tiffany would pick her up and babysit until Megan or Stephen got home from work.

Her thoughts were interrupted by Stephen's appearance in the open doorway of the connecting bathroom.

His eyes were shadowed in the low lighting afforded by her bedside lamp, and though she couldn't read his expression, her breath caught.

His tie hung loose around his neck. "Need some help?" he asked.

She dropped the bouquet of roses onto the bed. "Even if I did, asking you would be like asking a wolf to shepherd a lamb."

He flashed a smile and sauntered into the room. "Are you a lamb?" he murmured. "You're dressed in white…but not devoid of sin, from what I recall."

She tossed her hair, and moved to the bureau to remove her watch and earrings. "Spoken like a true scholar of the subject."

He laughed. "That's my girl."

"What do you want, Stephen?"

"In a word, you."

A tremor went through her at his words, despite her best attempts to steel herself against him. "Do I already need to remind you this is a marriage in name only?"

"I'm a patient man. I'm willing to wait for the pleasure of seeing you in that lingerie I sent you earlier in the week."

He moved up behind her and his hands clasped her shoulders. She stared at their image in the mirror in front of her.

She could feel the imprint of his body behind her, the male heat emanating from him and branding her. She picked up his masculine scent, one she recognized from four years ago and one which predictably awakened her senses.

He bent his head to nuzzle her neck, and her body reacted to remembered passion, as well as the image of the two of them together in the mirror.

His dark good looks were a perfect foil for her red hair and pale creamy skin.

His hands stroked up and down her arms, his mouth caressing the curve of her neck, then the shell of her ear...and the wisps of hair at her temple. Always teasing her.

Her nipples hardened, thrusting against the fabric of her gown.

She felt herself succumbing to him with mind-numbing ease, pulled under by a seductive undertow.

She turned in his arms, breaking free and intent on telling him off, but his mouth claimed hers before she could speak.

His lips moved over hers, taking control of the kiss, slipping past her barriers to touch her tongue with his and invite her to duel with him. Mate with him.

Her defenses came crashing down as the past

stormed back to greet them in all its passion and unfettered need.

His mouth moved over hers with greater urgency, and his hands roamed her back, bringing her closer to the flame of his desire.

She felt his erection press against her.

Sexual need ate at her. It was even hotter than before. Even hotter than she remembered.

She felt his hand at her back, tugging the zipper of her gown downward.

With a last desperate effort, she pulled her mouth from his and pushed away from him.

He took deep breaths, his eyes dilated from arousal.

Her breaths matched his, and she ached all over. Especially in her heart.

She hugged the sagging bodice of her dress to her.

He reached for her again, and she took a step back.

"You can't deny we both want it," he said in a quiet voice.

She raised her chin. "I'm wise enough to know now that *wanting* doesn't mean *having*."

They locked eyes, and she watched his expression shutter.

"One of these days, you're going to realize you're not the only one who's changed in the past four years," he said evenly.

They both stood there for a moment, not moving, before he strode out of the room.

She watched him leave, fighting to slow her pulse. Then she turned toward the vanity table to pick up her brush—and the broken pieces of her shattered four-year-old control.

Stephen arrived home on Monday to relieve the babysitter. He and Megan had decided to try out staggering their workdays as much as possible so that one of them would almost always be with Jade and they'd use their babysitter only to fill in small gaps.

"Hi, Stephen," Tiffany said, giving him a bright smile.

The sitter couldn't be more than twenty-two or twenty-three, he'd concluded when he'd first met her. Today, she wore hip-hugging denim shorts and a sleeveless tee with the words Baby Phat in rhinestones across the chest. Her straight blond hair was pulled back in a ponytail.

He was familiar with Tiffany's type. Women like her roamed at the periphery of his world—through the Garrison Grand's celebrity-hosted events, and at hot spots like his brother's nightclub, Estate.

"Hey," he said in acknowledgment. "Everything go okay today?"

Tiffany nodded, looking a little tongue-tied, and Stephen recognized the reaction. In some ways he was even used to it.

He wasn't a movie star or rock sensation, but with

his looks and wealth, he'd inspired reactions ranging from no-holds-barred come-ons to stolen glances and coy smiles. As the owner of the Garrison Grand, he was considered the epitome of cool—as much as it amused him sometimes.

Like everyone else, Tiffany had reacted with surprise when he and Megan had announced they were getting married. Still, she seemed to accept the explanation Megan had given—that the two of them had realized when they'd reencountered each other that they wanted to be together.

If Tiffany had caught on that he and Megan had begun their marriage sleeping in separate beds, she hadn't said anything. And frankly, Tiffany's presence was another reason he'd put Megan in the room next to his—aside from the obvious one of wanting Megan close by. He didn't want the babysitter to be the source of idle gossip. There'd been enough speculation out there among the public and the press about his lifestyle.

He loosened his tie just as Jade bounded into the room, holding what he'd come to know was her Baby Alive doll.

"Hello, gorgeous." He crouched and opened his arms, and Jade threw herself into them.

He'd recently been instructed by his daughter, in a very important voice, about all the cool characteristics of Baby Alive.

He seemed to recall Brittany and Brooke having a similar doll when they were little—one that, as a prank, he'd put in the pool to see if it could swim—so the toy apparently had staying power. Go figure.

He also decided it was best if he didn't mention that particular prank to Jade—though his sisters might rat him out at some point. Old stunts like that could tarnish his budding reputation as a great dad.

After a moment, Jade pulled back from his embrace. "Hi," she said, somewhat shyly.

He noticed that, despite her initial exuberance, Jade seemed to be hesitant.

One step forward, two steps back, he thought. But he was in this for the long haul.

After Tiffany left, he and Jade played with some puzzles and simple board games in the den until Megan arrived home.

They went out to greet her in the foyer.

One look at Megan, and his body tightened, the way it always did around her.

A short brown skirt showed off her spectacular legs, which were accentuated by stone-embellished spike-heeled sandals. She was wearing a short-sleeved blouse with a tropical print and gold chandelier earrings.

"Mommy!"

"Hi, sweetie." Megan's eyes traveled from Jade to him, a question in her eyes. "How are you doing?"

"We were just playing board games," he supplied.

Games a lot simpler than the one he and Megan were playing.

He reached out to take her upper arm and swept Megan's lips with a kiss. Jade, he noticed, absorbed it all with interest.

"Come on," he said to both of them. "I grill some mean steaks."

"Hamburger," Jade responded.

He feigned a long-suffering sigh. "All right, hamburger for you." He touched her nose. "But only because I feel like playing short-order cook tonight."

"What's a short-order cook?" Jade asked.

He slanted her a look. "Anyone cooking for someone who can barely reach the light switch."

Jade giggled.

He guided the little girl forward with his hand on her shoulder. "Come on, I'll explain."

"I'll join you as soon as I change," Megan said from behind them.

He turned back to her, quirking a brow. "Need some help?"

The air crackled with energy.

"No, thank you," she said, looking at him disapprovingly.

He flashed her a wicked smile. "Your choice."

"Yes."

"But I'm hoping to win the lottery one of these days."

She gave him a quelling look before heading for the stairs.

Later, they wound up having dinner on the patio, where they were able to watch the lowering sun. He grilled on his outdoor range, and Jade got her wish when he served up a Cuban-style burger seasoned with chorizo.

Jade's questions and requests peppered the dinner conversation, and Stephen realized this was what he should expect from now on.

They were a little family, the three of them, he thought, and it felt good. More than good.

It should have taken him longer to adjust from being a practiced playboy with honed predatory skills to protective father and husband. But instead it felt like coming home.

After dinner, he and Megan sat back and watched Jade explore and play on the patio.

"You're good with her," she remarked.

He leaned back farther in his chair. "She seemed a little hesitant when I came home today, though."

"That's natural."

He looked over at Jade. "Yeah, but I'm wondering whether something more is going on."

When Jade eventually came back over to join them, Megan leaned toward her. "Did you have a good day today, sweetie?"

Jade nodded, hopping back into her chair and taking a drink from her cup.

"Did you have fun at preschool?"

"Yes."

"Did something happen at school?" Megan prompted some more.

This time, Jade looked at him from the corner of her eyes.

"Jade?"

Jade looked down at her now-empty plate, and said in a rush, "I told Emily I had a daddy because you got married. She said no, I had a *stepfather*."

Oh, damn, Stephen thought.

He looked at Megan. It seemed as though their conversation with Jade was upon them faster than they'd anticipated.

Megan opened her mouth, but Stephen silenced her with a look.

"Jade, I *am* your daddy," he explained gently. "I was away for a little while, but I'm here now and will love you forever."

Jade looked up at him, such hopefulness in her eyes, it almost killed him.

"Do you understand?" he asked.

The little girl nodded. "Uh-huh."

"And even if I was your stepfather, I wouldn't love you any less."

Jade blinked, then blurted, "Can I call you Daddy?"

His heart did a weird twist.

"Of course," he said, his voice coming out unexpectedly hoarse.

"You'll never know how much I regret not being around when you were a baby," he said.

Jade got down from her chair and threw her arms around him.

His eyes met Megan's over Jade's dark head, and he thought he saw a sheen of tears in them.

Nine

On Saturday, Stephen took them out on his yacht, a sixty-foot Sea Ray.

Jade had pleaded to see the boat, and though Megan had her suspicions about how her daughter had gotten the idea in her head, she gave in.

Stephen had been so good with Jade this past week. The three of them had even toured the Garrison Grand early one evening, seeing the suite that Stephen kept there for his—now their—personal use. She couldn't deny him or her daughter the fun of an outing on Biscayne Bay.

From what she remembered, the yacht, named *Fishful Thinking,* was Stephen's prized possession.

The two of them had spent many carefree hours on it, making love and just relaxing and enjoying each other…until she'd discovered she wasn't the only woman he'd been entertaining aboard.

Now, as she stood in the stateroom, running a brush through her hair near a small mirror, she pushed the uncomfortable thought aside.

Stephen had killed the engine and dropped anchor so that the boat bobbed in the water.

After she and Stephen had taken turns diving and swimming off the side of the boat, they'd had lunch. Then Jade—worn out by the excitement of being on a yacht for the first time—had lain down for a nap.

Her daughter was asleep now on the bunk in the guest stateroom, so there was no innocent little girl around to run interference between her and Stephen. Megan sought to quell the nervousness that seized her.

As if conjured by her thoughts, Stephen appeared. He looked relaxed, fit and tanned in swim trunks and a short-sleeved navy T-shirt he'd donned after his swim.

"Hey, there," he said, resting his hand on the top of the door frame.

"Hi." She hated that he looked so at ease when she was a bundle of nerves. She'd intentionally put on a short skirt over her halter-top emerald bathing suit, but she still felt exposed.

It didn't help she'd seen amusement in the depths of Stephen's eyes when she'd done so, as if he saw right through her maneuver.

Now, as he looked her up and down, her body hummed in reaction. She prayed her nipples wouldn't harden, betraying her even more.

Despite the ease with which he'd assumed a fatherly role in Jade's life, she had to remember he was a rat and their relationship was *all business,* including this marriage.

"What are you doing?" he asked.

"Trying to get some knots out of my hair." Her hair had dried from her dip in the water earlier, but despite having had it in a ponytail, it had gotten tangled by the wind and water.

He continued to watch her with the same searing gaze he'd had when she'd stripped down to her bathing suit earlier.

"Jade wants to learn how to swim," she blurted.

His lips curved in the lopsided smile that never failed to send heat shooting through her. "I want to teach her. If she'd grown up here, near the water, she might already know how."

Surprisingly, she couldn't detect a hint of reproach in his voice. "She'd love to learn."

He stepped forward. "Here, let me help you."

She lowered the hand with the brush to her side.

"What?" she asked, though she'd heard him perfectly well. Her mind had just stopped at the image of Stephen touching her hair.

He grasped her wrist and gently removed the brush from her nerveless fingers. Then he stepped behind her, and she felt the movement of thick bristles from her scalp to the curling edges of her wavy hair.

She also felt his presence as he shifted against her—saw it in the small mirror in front of her—and her pulse picked up.

His skin gave off the scent of fresh air, salty water and sunscreen—and healthy male sweat.

They stood in silence. He lifted first one lock of hair, then another, pulling the brush through from root to tip.

She felt the air around her grow hot and heavy, until she had to concentrate on keeping her breathing even.

"Just like a mermaid," he murmured, arranging one curling edge over her shoulder before lifting another section of hair.

"No fins," she said automatically, and couldn't believe how breathless she sounded.

He chuckled, then sobered.

"I've been thinking about your accusation, and I've done some research," he said. "I looked back over my business diary from four years ago to try to refresh my memory about the night you were talking about."

She stiffened. "I'm surprised you didn't attempt hypnosis."

He laughed shortly before going on. "We hosted a party that night for an up-and-coming British rock group, and there were plenty of celebrity hangers-on involved. The woman you saw that night was there on a lark. She must have followed me back from the Garrison Grand, or gotten a tip from someone there that I owned a yacht."

"I wonder how she could have gotten the impression you were open to a brief encounter," she remarked acerbically.

He didn't react, apparently refusing to be baited by her sarcasm. "I admit I had a reputation as a player, and since you weren't around that night, someone thought I was fair game."

"I bet," she said unbendingly.

"But I did not sleep with that bottle blonde," he continued inexorably. "She sneaked aboard, but I sent her packing the second it became clear why she was there."

"How do you explain the fact she was still straightening her clothing when I saw her?" Megan asked. She didn't want to give him a chance to clarify things, but curiosity got the better of her.

In the mirror, she saw Stephen's lips twist. "I'm betting she saw you coming—maybe even recognized you—and decided to put on a show out of spite."

She finally felt herself relax a little at his words, despite her best intentions.

"You already think I'm a cheater," he said, as if

reading her mind. "I'm not about to compound my problems by becoming a liar, too."

"How do I know you won't cheat now?" she asked, her eyes meeting his in the mirror. "You're still the head of the Garrison Grand and—" she gestured around her "—you've still got this yacht. Women will want to come on to you."

He showed her the hand with his wedding ring. "This is your insurance."

She looked at his plain platinum band. "A wedding ring isn't considered an obstacle by some women."

"I just admitted that *at the time* you met me I had a reputation—"

She raised her eyebrows. "Really? The fact that you had to jog your memory speaks volumes." Though her words were sharp, it was getting hard to maintain her edge when he was practically giving her a scalp massage. "You couldn't even remember the woman who showed up that night."

"But I could never forget you," he said against her temple. "That's why I turned her away."

She felt his words with shattering force. Her walls where he was concerned—never sturdy to begin with—crumbled some more.

"I want to make love," he stated, and her insides turned to mush.

"That's not a good idea," she managed to say through a constricted throat.

"On the contrary," he responded, tossing the brush aside. "I think it's the best idea I've had in a *long* time."

He spun her around to face him, and her hands fell against his chest.

He dipped his head, and his mouth plundered hers.

Tongues touched and lips moved, shifted, caressed, and just like that, the dam burst.

She moaned low in her throat.

His fingers delved into her hair, undoing his handiwork as he pulled her head back. His mouth skimmed along the side of her neck.

"I want you so damn much," he muttered.

Her hands moved to grip his shoulders, anchoring herself in a world gone topsy-turvy.

When his mouth met the obstacle of her bathing suit, his fingers went to the clasp of the halter top and released the bonds that kept her from him. Her breasts spilled forward, and his hands came up to palm and stroke them, rubbing folds of nylon across sensitized nipples.

The force of their desire came roaring to life, the way it always had.

They couldn't get enough of each other. Mouth fused to mouth, and his hands shot down, skimming under her skirt to grasp her buttocks and bring her flush against him to feel the strength of his need.

The past had been a glorious ride before she'd been thrown, but it had brought her Jade, and now suddenly she wanted to reach out again with both hands to grasp the sunshine, feeling reckless—no, feeling like a gambler.

She felt the strong beat of his heart and felt the thrilling excitement of wanting to be joined with him.

Her skirt hit the floor, and their hands roamed with increasing urgency. Her fingers stroked and delved, retracing every luscious inch of him that had been imprinted on her memory.

During the years they'd been apart, she'd still dreamed about him—fantasized about him. It hadn't mattered that she'd thought he was a cheat. Her heart at night was free to roam where her mind would not allow itself to go when she was awake.

Now, he pulled away from her and yanked his shirt over his head, exposing a chest she'd itched to touch ever since he'd stripped down to his bathing trunks for their swim earlier.

Her fingers danced over defined muscle, until she gave in to the urge to place openmouthed kisses where her hands had just been. His skin tasted warm, salty and sun-kissed.

With an oath of frustration, he bent and pulled down his swim trunks.

His impressive erection sprang free, exciting her even more.

She quivered, her body tightening—a reaction that echoed those she'd felt whenever they were together.

"I've got to have you," he said, and her senses ran riot.

He hooked his thumbs under the fabric of her swimsuit and pulled it off her.

His mouth came down to ravage hers. After a moment, he hooked his foot behind her ankle, sliding her leg forward and throwing her off balance so they both tumbled onto the bed next to them.

He feasted on her breasts, then found all her pleasure points: the hollow behind her ear…the curve of her breast…her inner thigh…her instep. All the while she did a slow slide to mindless desire.

And still he played with her.

He was a master at bringing her vibrantly to life.

She raked her hands down his back as he kissed her hip bone, then the indentation it formed.

When he touched her welcoming wetness with his hand, she sucked in a breath, tensing.

"Relax," he murmured.

How could she relax when she could hear the dark intent in his voice? She could feel his breath against her, and her pulse accelerated.

The first touch of his mouth sent waves of sensation surging through her.

"Stephen."

He growled against her damp heat, then delved in to pleasure her with his mouth.

She turned her head toward the mattress, her hands grasping the sheets.

She moaned, sighed and careened toward release. Within moments, she trembled against him before sinking back against the mattress, weak and fulfilled.

Seconds later, she watched as he moved up next to her and looked over at a nearby drawer. "Damn it. I just realized I don't have any protection."

"I haven't been with anyone since our affair." She was desperate for him, otherwise she'd never have been so direct. Her body was still wet and wanting.

He looked at her questioningly, then his eyes kindled.

"With a small child, there hasn't been time for anything," she explained.

"I'm healthy," he said.

She nodded.

"But you could get pregnant," he went on, holding her gaze.

Her heart flipped. "Or not. It's the wrong time of the month."

The truth was there were times when she'd been sad that Jade might not have any siblings. She'd foreclosed other possibilities when she'd married Stephen. *Why not take this?* her heart whispered.

"We're married," he said, his erection resting against her. "This time it's you and me in it together, either way."

"We've already made that bargain," she responded in a low voice, though she knew another child hadn't factored into their arrangement.

Her green light was the last encouragement he needed.

His mouth claimed hers, and with his lead, their need for each other was stoked to a blistering height once more.

When he finally sank into her, she expelled a breath on a long sigh.

"I know, baby," he murmured, soothing her. "Let me give you what you want—what we both need."

She caught his rhythm as effortlessly as she always had. It was a dance they'd always performed well, moving with primal instinct.

He thrust, sending her higher and higher. She clung to him, moaning, reaching, and leaving herself open to feeling.

Then, just when she thought the tension couldn't build up anymore, the coil within her released, and she shattered.

She felt him strain back, thrust one final time, and with a guttural groan, climax after her.

"Everyone, this is Jade," Stephen said, his hand resting on his daughter's shoulder.

Stephen's siblings stepped forward in turn to greet Jade.

Megan wet her lips nervously.

All the Garrisons had gathered, including Parker and Anna. Anna had said she'd show up to give moral support, and now Megan was glad for it.

Though Stephen's family had seen Jade at the wedding, this Sunday-night dinner at the Garrison estate would be their first opportunity to really interact with her.

This was also her own very first visit to the Bal Harbour estate, Megan reflected. She'd never stepped inside Stephen's parents' mansion during their fling, but she was here now as his wife and the mother of their child.

She let her gaze travel over her surroundings with a designer's practiced eye. The foyer was designed to impress—intimidate even—as was the entire estate.

The double-height foyer was dominated by an immense stone fireplace, before which were arranged various armchairs and sofas. Thick stone Corinthian columns supported graceful archways. To one side, a wide stone staircase led to a second level, where a gallery, bracketed by more stone columns, ran around the perimeter of the room and gave a glimpse of the rooms on the upper level.

Four years ago, she'd met all the Garrison siblings at one event or another. Parker, of course, she'd worked for, and she and Stephen had partied at

Adam's nightclub, where she'd also met the twins, Brittany and Brooke.

She wished, however, that she'd also met Stephen's mother back then. The matriarch of the clan had greeted her stiffly at the wedding and now held back, surveying the scene.

When all of Stephen's siblings had stopped fussing over Jade, Stephen's mother looked down at her granddaughter.

"Come here, little girl," Bonita said, and after a slight hesitation, Jade stepped forward.

Megan could feel Stephen tense beside her.

She'd dressed Jade in a sleeveless emerald-green dress, tying her daughter's hair back with a ribbon. She'd wanted Jade to make the best impression possible. She could deal with rejection for herself, but she wanted Jade to be accepted—embraced even—by the Garrisons.

So far, to her relief, all of Stephen's siblings had reacted warmly, surpassing expectations that she'd tried to keep in check so as not to be disappointed.

Now, though, she held her breath as Bonita grasped Jade's chin and tilted her face up so she could examine the little girl's face.

Seconds ticked by, and Megan felt as if everyone else in the room was holding their breath right along with her.

"There's no mistaking the fact you're a Garrison," Bonita stated finally. "The image of your father, in fact."

Though there was no visible softening of Bonita's features, everyone seemed to relax slightly. The lack of censure in Bonita's voice made it likely this evening at least might pass without incident.

"I'm your grandmother," Bonita said. "You may call me Grandmother."

Bonita dropped her hand, and Jade nodded, wide-eyed.

Megan's shoulders lowered. Stephen had filled her in on the fact that Bonita had a drinking problem that had become exacerbated recently. She'd stated that his mother could prove difficult about accepting what were, in her view, a mistress and out-of-wedlock child into the family.

Yet, it seemed Bonita's affection for her son had won the day, and Megan felt her tension ebb some more.

As people began to mingle and talk, waiting for dinner to be served in the dining room, Stephen moved away to speak with Adam, and Brittany approached her.

Stephen's sister squeezed her arm. "I'm so happy for you and Stephen."

Megan put a smile on her face. "Thanks, and likewise for you and Emilio." She looked over Brittany's shoulder. "Where is he by the way?"

Brittany laughed. "Busy with El Diablo."

Megan nodded. "He must work hard. That restaurant has gotten great reviews for its food and ambience."

Brittany leaned in. "Between you and me, I think it's just as well he isn't here. We're still easing our way with the family."

"Tell me about it," she responded ruefully. "I was nervous about coming tonight. Everyone had to be on their best behavior for the wedding, but tonight is a different matter."

"You're doing great," Brittany said, then looked across the room at Stephen. "You know, I suspected Stephen was carrying a torch for you after your breakup."

Megan felt a flutter, but then reminded herself that Brittany was hardly an impartial party.

"Not our playboy action hero," she said glibly.

"He matured, too," Brittany insisted. "Since you left, he built up the Garrison Grand even more. I think he poured himself into it, and in the process, he took a good hotel and made it great."

"I can't disagree there," Megan murmured, looking across the room now, too. Stephen had studied her plans for the hotel's conference and business center and made some modifications to make the renovation even more state-of-the-art. She had to admit he knew his stuff.

"My only concern was that he was becoming just a little too focused and ruthless," Brittany went on, turning to look at her again. "Now that he's married, I can stop worrying."

If only Brittany knew the half of it, Megan thought.

Of course, Brittany wanted to believe she and Stephen had found a happily-ever-after—she was in love herself. From what Stephen had told her before the wedding, Megan knew Brittany was newly engaged to Emilio Jefferies and planning a splashy wedding.

But she also knew her own situation was far different. Stephen's ruthlessness hadn't ebbed a bit, and she and Stephen had married for convenience.

She almost blurted out the latter to Brittany, but she contented herself with saying, "Jade's certainly had an effect on him."

After Stephen's sister had moved off to speak with her twin, Megan found herself mulling over the weekend's events.

Yesterday, when they'd gotten home from their outing on the yacht and put Jade to bed, she'd fallen asleep herself atop her own bed. After changing into her sleep tee, she'd meant to lie down only for a few minutes before doing some work-related reading. Instead, in the morning, she'd woken up under some blankets. She'd realized Stephen must have come in at some point and covered her up, and a wave of awareness had washed over her, despite her best efforts.

Then today, she and Stephen had both been so

busy with Jade, there'd been no time to talk. In many ways, though, she'd been grateful for the distraction.

True, yesterday the sex between her and Stephen had been fantastic. Their unbridled need had proven to her once again that, where Stephen Garrison was concerned, she had no self-control.

Yet though she believed Stephen's explanation of what had happened—or, rather, what had *not* happened—that night four years ago on his boat, she wasn't sure what they had between them now was more than just good sex.

Yes, he wanted her back in his life, but it was because he thought the two of them should raise Jade together. He wanted to be fully involved in his daughter's life, and the only way to do that was to include Jade's mother in a package deal.

Undeniably, on the yacht yesterday, she'd had a moment of recklessness that might have made her pregnant again—though the possibility was unlikely. At least this time, though, she was married and had already committed to raising one child with Stephen.

But she knew better than to risk her heart again. Stephen had never said he loved her, and given the long line of women in his life—despite Brittany's claim about his newfound maturity—she doubted he ever would. She might be the most memorable in his long line of conquests, but he'd given her no reason to believe she'd ever been more.

Still, because she'd rejected him four years ago, he saw her as a sexual challenge now. She belatedly realized she'd all but waved the red flag in front of him when she'd announced she wouldn't sleep with him.

Stephen had a strong sex drive, and she was his wife. If no longer in name only, she reminded herself, still just out of convenience.

Ten

Stephen had the chance to speak to his mother alone after the family dinner. He stopped her at the base of the foyer staircase.

Good thing that today she seemed more sober than usual. Still, he had a good hunch she'd been heading upstairs to her stash of liquor.

"You're out of control," he said without preamble.

She raised an eyebrow haughtily. "Excuse me, but I have no idea what you mean."

He had to give his mother credit. Even struggling with an addiction to alcohol, she was still the grand dame. But he knew where the truth lay.

"Let's dispense with the subterfuge," he said.

If possible, Bonita seemed to freeze even more. "I'm your mother. I won't have you speaking to me this way."

With her hand on the railing, Bonita took a step up, but he placed his hand over hers, halting her progress.

"I'm talking about your drinking, Mother. It's started to affect the entire family, and it's consuming your life."

Bonita straightened, her spine stiffening with outrage. "How dare you? Wasn't I polite and cordial to your wife and daughter? Didn't I welcome them into my home?"

"Your drinking is upsetting the whole family," he continued implacably.

Bonita's eyes snapped with anger. "How dare you speak to me about *upsetting* this family? Your father cheated and imperiled the family fortune, and you've decided to follow in his footsteps."

He sighed. The family peace that had prevailed tonight appeared to be over. He'd figured Megan would come into this at one point or another.

"Your accusations are off the mark. I didn't cheat on my wife—" Though Megan had thought he'd cheated on her before they were married, he decided his mother didn't need to know about a false accusation "—and I sure didn't jeopardize the family fortune. Parker and I are working to get this situation with the woman in the Bahamas straightened out. The *only* parallel with Dad is that I had a child out of wedlock, but I don't regret Jade's existence for a second."

His mother's lips thinned. "And now your mistress has joined the family, too. You outdid your father in that department, Stephen."

He held on to Bonita's hand when she tried to ascend. "Make no mistake, Mother. Megan *is* part of this family, and she's here to stay. I won't tolerate your being rude to her."

Then because of his purpose in seeking out his mother tonight, and because he could read the turbulence and pain in her eyes unusually well at the moment, he softened his voice. "Get yourself some help, Mother. Otherwise, we'll have to do it for you."

After a tense moment during which neither of them spoke, Bonita extricated her hand from his and went up the stairs without a look back.

Watching his mother depart, Stephen reflected on her accusations, and his thoughts naturally turned to the status of his relationship with Megan.

Yesterday had been fantastic. He'd taken Megan and Jade for an outing aboard his prized yacht and had been able to share one of his favorite pastimes with his daughter for the first time. Life didn't get any better.

On top of it all, his and Megan's lovemaking had been as explosive as ever. He meant to repeat the experience as soon as possible. Tonight, if he could arrange it.

Yesterday, when Megan hadn't seemed to mind the possibility of getting pregnant again, he'd nearly blown his cool right then with his blinding need to have her.

Now, the thought of having more children with her made his pulse quicken all over again. This time he wanted to be around for all of it. He wanted to experience the wonder of pregnancy with her. He wanted to be there when their child was born.

He wanted Megan in his bed, in his life. Period.

If Megan didn't realize it already, he was going to set out to prove it to her.

Their marriage in name only was about to become a marriage in every possible way.

When they got home from Bonita's estate, Megan helped Jade get ready for bed, then tiptoed out of her daughter's room while Stephen read a bedtime story.

Returning to her own room, she thought about how wonderful it would be to luxuriate in a warm bath for half an hour. She'd survived the evening, and all she wanted to do now was relax.

Instead, however, she opted for a quick shower in the adjoining bathroom. A hot shower would do the trick almost as well to relieve her tight muscles. And it had the added benefit of being relatively fast—no need to worry too much about Stephen moving around in the next room.

She stripped, then walked into the bathroom and got the water running in the shower. Stepping into the stall, she sighed and closed her eyes as hot jets of water pounded her.

All in all, she had to admit the evening hadn't gone *badly*. Bonita—judging from what Stephen had told her beforehand by way of warning—seemed to have behaved fairly well.

And Stephen's siblings had been warm, welcoming and nonjudgmental. They appeared to accept that whatever her relationship with Stephen had been, and whatever reasons she'd had for not telling Stephen about Jade, it was all water under the bridge now that she and Stephen were married.

She sighed again.

"Need me to do your back?"

She gasped and jerked around.

Stephen stood outside the shower stall, and from his lazy, amused tone, he'd gotten quite an eyeful.

"What are you doing here?" Surprise made her tone sharp.

His lopsided grin emerged. "I knocked on your bedroom door, and when I got no response, I came in." His eyes crinkled. "I thought you might have fallen asleep on the bed—again."

"Well, as you can see, I'm taking a shower!"

His eyes traveled downward. "Yeah, I can see all right—"

"What do you want?"

His eyes came back to hers. "Take a guess."

She regretted her choice of words. "I'll be out soon."

She made her tone repressive. They needed to talk, that was for sure—but not here and now! She used her pointed tone to mask her susceptibility.

She felt vulnerable and exposed, not to mention that standing before him naked was doing strange things to her insides.

Stephen's grin only widened. "Sure about the back scrub?"

"No, thanks."

· "I'll try to get over the devastating rejection."

"I know it doesn't happen much, but join the masses."

His eyes glinted at her humor. "Do you remember the showers we took together?" he murmured. "We'd wind up late for work."

She certainly *hadn't* forgotten. How could she? She'd replayed those scenes in her mind too many times over the years.

She moved to turn off the shower. "I've grown up," she responded.

"So have I," he drawled, turning toward the door, "but that doesn't exclude indulging in some fun."

Judging by their encounter yesterday, she'd have to agree with him. Mercifully, though, she was spared a response as he walked out of the room.

* * *

Twenty minutes later, she wandered downstairs in her bare feet, a satin robe over a matching knee-length gown. Damp tendrils of hair lay against her shoulders. She hadn't completely succeeded in keeping her hair dry despite tying it up for the shower.

She found Stephen in the spacious living room. The lights were turned down low, and the voice of Harry Connick, Jr. crooning "Only You" sounded softly in the background.

Stephen stood holding two wineglasses filled with red wine. He held one out to her.

A little flame she was all too familiar with ignited inside her.

She'd sought him out for a talk—the recent episode in the shower had convinced her they were past due for one—but this wasn't quite the ambience she was expecting.

"Relax," he said, as if reading her mind.

She realized her only hope rested with appearing cool and nonchalant. Stephen would exploit any hint of responsiveness to his advantage.

With that thought, she took the wineglass from him—ignoring how the brush of their hands sent a tingling through her—and sat with him on the couch.

"Thanks for coming to the family dinner tonight," he said. "I know it was stressful for you."

"It's important for Jade to meet your family," she

said, glad to be on a safe topic. "She is the first grand-child, after all."

She took a sip of her drink. She'd expected him to immediately begin putting the moves on her, so he'd thrown her off with his comment.

Still, it was hard not to be aware of him. He was impossibly masculine in black pants and an open-collar white shirt. His shirtsleeves had been rolled back to expose the dark hair of his arms.

Now, he nodded. "I know some of my siblings would have bet good money against my being the father of the first grandchild. We almost beat Parker and Anna to the altar, too."

She looked down into her glass. "Your mother behaved well."

She hadn't gotten a warm, fuzzy feeling from Bonita Garrison, but she was happy the woman had been polite and accepting of Jade.

"For a change," Stephen said.

She looked up at him again. "Do you ever worry about drinking yourself?"

He shook his head. "No, I set clear limits to when I'll drink, and I can stick to them. Besides—" he shot her a significant look "—I get into enough trouble without bringing alcohol into it."

She knew he was thinking about their relationship and, specifically, about the child they'd produced.

"You haven't told me about your years in India-napolis," he said abruptly.

She shrugged. "There isn't much to tell. I was raising a child with help from my family."

She talked then about her life in Indiana. She told him about her family and friends, and the funny little things that had happened to her.

"How did you support yourself?" he asked.

"I did small contract jobs for family, friends and neighbors." She shrugged again. "You know, helping someone remodel a kitchen or add on to a house."

His lips tightened.

"I know what you're thinking," she said. "Don't say it."

"We're married now," he responded. "That's what counts."

"Yes, about that—"

She wet her lips, then stopped as she saw he'd focused on the action.

"Are you going to express regrets about accusing me of cheating?" His eyes held hers steadily. "You should have faced me four years ago with your suspicions."

"I was wrong not to face you," she admitted, knowing she owed him that, at least. "You'll never know how many times I've wondered over the years whether I made the right decision for Jade."

He looked mollified.

She took a deep breath. "But I've also come to

the realization that meeting that woman that night was just the catalyst for my leaving. I knew what your life was like—"

His brows snapped together.

"—and we were having a no-strings affair."

He leaned forward to place his wineglass on the end table. "Oh, there were strings, baby, make no mistake about it."

She put down her wineglass, too, and rose. "That's why yesterday shouldn't set a pattern."

He got to his feet, too. "I agree."

"You do?" She couldn't keep the surprise from her voice. Well, *that* was easy.

His arms snaked around her. "Next time, it's going to be dry land or nothing. A small cabin like that isn't big enough for our kind of—" his eyes gleamed "—physically demanding lovemaking."

She nearly choked.

"Hey, I'm a *big* guy."

This time, she did splutter, but she could see from the amusement on his face that he was enjoying toying with her—enjoying having her wonder exactly what he meant by *big*.

A smile teased his lips. "Four years ago, we were closer to being kids. We could have made do with a park bench. Now, as you've pointed out, we're seeing the wrong side of thirty."

"I said *I* was grown-up—"

His head came down, and he claimed her mouth.

Behind her eyelids, the world erupted in color. Her mind swam.

Pressing his advantage, he plundered her mouth, making her open to him. Making her feel.

She moaned low in her throat, even as a part of her mind fought for control.

After several moments, she tore her mouth from his. "Stephen—"

In response, he bent her backward, and her robe fell open. He trailed his lips down her throat, lingering over the pulse under her jaw.

Pulsating awareness sang through her veins and gathered at the juncture of her thighs.

Oh. "We have to talk—"

"Trust me on this one, Meggikins," he said thickly. "There are actions more valuable than words right now."

"I'm not sure that's the saying," she said somewhat breathlessly, raising her head. He used to call her Meggikins all the time before she left Miami. This was the first time he'd used her old nickname in his previous sweet, unsarcastic way.

"Whatever," he responded. "There are times when we guys call it right."

He was getting it more than right, she thought. He was playing her like a virtuoso handling a Stradivarius.

He stared at the silky nightgown revealed by her

open robe. She could tell he'd focused on her nipples, which had tightened and now jutted against the thin material of her gown.

His eyes darkened, his face growing taut with desire. "Do you know I fantasized about you?" He shook his head slowly. "It used to drive me crazy that I kept thinking about you when you'd been the one to walk away."

"That's why you want me now. I'm a novelty. The one who dumped you." She guessed this wasn't the time to tell him she'd dreamed about him, too. It would be like adding fuel to the fire. She could feel his erection pressed against her.

He shook his head again, his brows coming together. He gave her a little shake. "Don't give me that garbage. You're the mother of my child."

Her heart plummeted, even as she told herself she shouldn't care whether he saw her as just a mother or not at all.

"We can barely be in the same room without wanting to get it on," he said huskily.

Her heart skipped a beat. "Lust."

"Sexual attraction," he contradicted. "It's more than a lot of other people have."

But it wasn't enough for her. "What happens when it all fades?"

"It hasn't in four years."

She shook her head in denial.

His eyes gleamed. "Do you need me to show you again just how much it can be worth?"

His hand skimmed up her thigh, raising her gown and robe. His head lowered.

"We shouldn't," she whispered.

"What?" he muttered against her mouth. "We're married. We're legal. We're not inebriated."

"This isn't what I signed up for."

"Hell, me, too, but sometimes you just have to run with it."

He hoisted her up and fastened his mouth to hers.

Oh, damn. She'd underestimated just how hard it would be to live under the same roof and resist him. And he wasn't making it any easier on her.

In the background, Harry Jr. had faded into the slow, sultry tones of Norah Jones.

Without breaking contact, Stephen used one hand to pull her panties off, then sat back on the couch with her.

Her legs came down on either side of him, straddling him.

He rubbed her sensitized nipples and made a guttural sound of pleasure.

Yes, her mind whimpered.

She'd gone so long without. So long without him. Yesterday, the dam had burst, and now all her desires came pouring forth.

He kissed her jaw, then pushed the robe off her shoulders so that it dropped to the floor. He kissed her neck, her shoulder and her collarbone, then gave her a little love bite.

She fumbled with the buttons of his shirt, sliding against him, needing him to fill the dull ache inside her.

Eventually, with a groan, he stilled her hands against his shirt. He grasped the bottom of her gown and pulled her last article of clothing over her head before tossing it aside.

Turning back to her, he reached between them. He delved, testing her with his fingers and finding her wetness.

And she savored his touch. Her eyes closed, her back arched, and her breathing became shallow. She clenched around him.

"That's right," he muttered. "Come to me, my mermaid."

She opened her eyes and looked at him.

From the harsh, intent look on his face, she knew he was ready. *She* was ready.

He withdrew his hand, and with quivering fingers, she helped him undo his belt and free himself.

She held his gaze as she sank down on him, joining them and making them both sigh with pleasure.

She rode him then with sweet rhythm while he whispered encouragement in her ear.

Slowly, slowly, they climbed to the pinnacle together.

When she peeked at him and saw his jaw was

locked, she realized only iron control kept him from taking her wildly. She knew he was waiting for her—trying to make this good for her.

And with that awareness, all her nervous tension broke and she found a magnificent release.

He caught her when she came, taking over in the last few moments and thrusting up to meet her with a deep groan as he shook and strained one last time.

Eleven

On Friday, Megan met Anna for lunch at La Loggia, near Elkind, Ross's offices downtown.

After they'd ordered, Anna said, "Marriage seems to agree with you."

"Does it?" Megan remarked, lifting her water glass.

"Mmm-hmm," Anna persisted, a teasing light in her eyes. "You look as if you've been having lots of sex—and enjoying it."

She choked on a sip of water. *"What?"*

"Are you okay?" Anna responded, laughing.

"How would you know that?" She felt as if she were wearing an *H* for *horny* emblazoned on her knit top.

Anna gave another tinkling laugh. "Simple.

I'm married to a Garrison, too, and I'm also a newlywed."

Megan resisted the urge to cup her hot cheeks.

The past week had been crazy. She and Stephen were married parents of a young child, and they were conducting a passionate affair.

The couch…the desk…the breakfast table. They were sneaking around a three-year-old. They'd even put his gift of lingerie to good use.

Just last night, after they'd put Jade to bed, Stephen had bent her forward over the desk in his study and had intercourse with her.

Anna took a sip from her water glass, seemingly reading Megan's silence for the admission it was. "Mmm-hmm. Persuasive, was he?" she murmured.

Megan groaned and hid her face behind her hands.

"Oh, Anna," she said when she looked up, "we've been on a roller coaster this past week."

Her friend laughed again. "So you're having wild, uninhibited sex with your husband. What's wrong with that?"

Everything.

"He… We…"

Anna's lips twitched. "I understand. Stephen's an attractive guy with a healthy sex drive and he wanted to get it on with you."

Megan expelled a breath and nodded. "The rat. He's reneging on the terms of this marriage."

Her friend placed a hand over her heart melodramatically. "How? By wanting to have sex with you, his wife, rather than someone else?"

"When you put it that way, it sounds so reasonable."

"It *is* reasonable."

Rather than concede, however, she held on doggedly to her position, which she nevertheless knew was fast becoming unsustainable.

Still, she felt compelled to set the record straight on one score. "It turns out he wasn't having sex with anyone else four years ago, either."

Anna raised an eyebrow, and Megan recounted Stephen's story to her.

"And I believed him," she said when she finished.

"So," Anna said, "everything should be great now, right?"

She shook her head. "*No.* Don't you see?" she said, her voice almost a wail. "I was vulnerable to believing that woman four years ago because Stephen had such a reputation as a player, and nothing has changed, and—and, oh God, I may be falling for him again!"

Panic roiled her stomach.

She was in love with him. Maybe had always remained a little in love with him.

Anna patted her hand.

She looked at her sister-in-law, her eyes pleading. "Why, why, why did he have to insist on this marriage? We could have come to an arrangement that allowed him to see Jade!"

Anna shook her head. "Megan, Megan, look around!" Anna glanced to one side of them, then to the other. "Do you know how many men have looked over at us—at you—since we arrived? You're a tall, gorgeous redhead who attracts more attention than a neon sign in the desert. Of course Stephen wanted to slap a ring on your hand as soon as possible!"

Megan closed her eyes, sucked in some deep, controlling breaths, then looked at her friend again.

"You're fearful right now, that's all," Anna said. "Believe me, I understand. I was just there. Falling in love is scary. And then there are all those trust issues."

"I know," she said matter-of-factly.

Trust. Anna and Parker didn't have the lengthy tortured history she and Stephen did and yet Anna knew about the importance of that little word.

Just then, the waiter approached with their food.

All through lunch, however, Megan wondered about her new discovery and how she was going to handle it.

She was in love with Stephen Garrison. Again.

A storm was on the way. Stephen looked up at the sky from the deck of *Fishful Thinking*. Fortunately, the storm wasn't a hurricane—at least for now.

Still, it would hit over the weekend, and he wanted to make sure his yacht was prepared.

Though the staff at the marina could do the work for him, *Fishful Thinking* was his baby, and he liked to get personally involved when he could.

The yacht needed to be tied up with longer, sturdier lines, and as a precaution, he needed to clear out some of his personal possessions.

He headed below deck, then turned at the sound of someone clambering aboard.

Retracing his steps, he felt a smile rise to his lips. Megan was early.

They'd agreed last night to meet at the marina after work and have a Friday night out. He'd been looking forward to it all day.

But as he came up on deck again, he saw his visitor wasn't Megan, but their babysitter.

Tiffany was dressed as if she was heading out for a night on the town. She was wearing a sheer blouse, black miniskirt and heels, and her face was more made-up than usual.

He remembered now mentioning to the babysitter that he'd have to tie up his boat at the Miami Beach Marina after work today.

"What's up, Tiffany?" His thoughts automatically went to his daughter. "Is something wrong with Jade?" he asked, his voice coming out sharp.

"No, no, no," Tiffany said on a breathless laugh,

walking toward him. "I dropped her off at her friend Gillian's birthday party earlier."

He relaxed. "Well, if you're thinking you need to babysit, there are crossed wires. My sister-in-law, Anna, is supposed to pick her up from the party—" he consulted his watch "—in a little over an hour."

He and Megan had agreed Anna and Parker would take Jade for the evening while they went out for a quick dinner, just the two of them. Anna had been thrilled at the prospect of babysitting.

"No crossed wires," Tiffany said easily, her gaze focused on his face, "and there's plenty of time for what I came to discuss."

"Oh, yeah?"

She nodded to the stairs. "Can we talk somewhere more private?" She hugged herself and looked around. "It's windy out here."

"Yeah, with good reason. There's a storm coming ashore," he said, but nevertheless turned to lead the way.

"I've never been aboard before," Tiffany said from behind him once they were in the narrow corridor below deck. "Is this where you nap?"

He turned around to see Tiffany peering into the master cabin.

"Yup," he said, then braced his hands on his hips. He'd dressed in pants and an open-collar shirt for work today because he'd known he'd be heading over to the yacht to meet Megan for dinner. "Now why don't you tell me what this is about?"

Tiffany straightened and peeked up at him through her lashes. "Better yet, I'll show you."

She stepped forward and fastened her mouth to his.

It happened so fast, he didn't have a chance to react. In the tight confines of the yacht's passageway, there wasn't much room to move.

Still, it was the last thing he'd been expecting from Tiffany, so for a second he remained immobile.

She pressed closer, going up on tiptoe, her arms snaking around his neck.

"Mmm," she murmured.

As she moved her mouth over his, his brain snapped on. *What the hell.*

He reached for her arms and tugged them from his neck.

She touched his chest, looking up at him pleadingly. "Do me."

He opened his mouth, flabbergasted.

"Excuse me."

He and Tiffany both turned to look at the end of the passageway.

Megan stood rigidly, silhouetted by the light, then spun on her heel.

Stephen cursed. "Megan, wait!"

He started after her, but Tiffany fisted her hand into the back of his shirt, stopping him.

He turned back, his brows snapping together. "What the hell are you doing?"

"Let her go, Stephen."

"She's my wife!"

Tiffany smirked. "C'mon, I know you're not sleeping with her. She's been in the guest bedroom."

Oh, hell. Yes, Megan's stuff still remained in the guest bedroom, but he'd been having a damn good week, seducing Megan at every opportunity— making headway, or so he thought. And now this.

Tiffany trailed a hand down his chest. "I know a virile guy like you must have a difficult time doing without," she said, lowering her voice invitingly. "So, here I am."

He removed her hand from his chest. "You don't know a thing," he said coldly.

The first glimmer of uncertainty entered the babysitter's eyes. "C'mon, Stephen. Everyone knows you play the field—"

"Past tense there, honey." In fact, in the last couple of years, his reputation had been based more on past public perception than on reality.

He glowered at her. "What's your game?"

Tiffany affected a pout. "Nothing! You're one of the sexiest, hippest guys in Miami. Everyone knows about the Garrison brothers. I wanted to see what all the fuss was about."

Stephen sighed inwardly. He'd been reduced to a

notch on the bedpost, and the irony wasn't lost on him. Aloud, he said, "You're going to explain to Megan *exactly* what happened here."

"That we were kissing?" Tiffany smirked again. "I think she saw that for herself."

"No, that you came on to me unexpectedly."

Tiffany's jaw set mulishly. "I can't do that."

"You *can,* and you *will.*" He resisted the urge to shake some sense into her.

"If I say that, I'll never get another child-care job! I have to stick to the story it was mutual."

He was surprised and even a bit impressed at how much she'd thought this through. It made him wonder, though, just how many guys Tiffany had come on to in the past. He'd been at the receiving end of enough conniving women to be sort of jaded about the type.

"You won't get a job based on the recommendation I'd give you," he gritted.

She folded her arms. "At least my way I'll have a fighting chance. It'll be my word against yours."

Tiffany had cost him, and cost him big, with Megan, but Stephen suddenly felt an iota of sympathy for the babysitter. She was young and impressionable, and obviously looking for love in all the wrong places.

"Stop chasing a rainbow. Fame and being hip isn't all it's cracked up to be," he advised.

Then he turned away to try to find his wife.

* * *

Megan blindly found her way back to her car. She got behind the wheel and her brain went on automatic pilot as she steered out of the parking lot.

It was just like four years ago. A wild affair where she couldn't see straight, then blindsided by a betrayal.

She should have known. She should have known.

Once a cheater, always a cheater, the naysayer within her chanted.

She made herself relive the pain of catching Tiffany and Stephen in an intimate embrace.

At least four years ago she'd been spared the visual evidence. Then she'd gone only on the word of a woman she hadn't met before. *That,* and Stephen's playboy reputation.

This time, she'd witnessed the cheating herself.

As she made a left turn at a stoplight, she realized she couldn't go home—or rather, to Stephen's estate near South Beach. He'd be there, and she needed time to think.

Her cell phone rang, and she ignored it. She recognized the ring as Stephen's.

Her mind raced ahead. The Garrison Grand was also off-limits for obvious reasons. Under other circumstances, she might have turned to Anna for help, but Anna was now married to Stephen's brother.

With that thought, her mind went to Jade. At least

she wouldn't need to worry about her daughter tonight. She knew Anna would be happy to take care of Jade for as long as needed.

Her cell phone rang again, and she turned it off with one hand.

She realized after a moment that she could always go to the little house in Coral Gables. She had the lease until the end of the month, and some of her furniture and belongings were still in the house.

Her mind made up, she turned the car west.

A short time later, when she reached her former home, she let herself in, kicked off her sandals and turned her phone back on.

The screen on her cell flashed information on several missed calls from Stephen. Cynically, she wondered what explanation he'd come up with this time.

Then she searched for and found Anna's number. When her sister-in-law picked up, she said, "Anna, it's Megan."

"Hi! I was just about to go get Jade—"

"Listen, would you mind keeping her until tomorrow?"

"Of course I don't mind," Anna responded. "We'll just run by the Garrison Grand on the way home and pick up some stuff for her from your suite."

Like Stephen, Megan knew, Parker and Anna maintained a suite at the Garrison Grand for personal use.

"Thanks," Megan said, relief making her relax. "I

left some clothes over there when Jade got a tour of her father's hotel."

The father who had just proved once again he was a lying, cheating, untrustworthy rat.

"You and Stephen want the evening to yourselves, hmm?" Anna asked teasingly.

"Something like that." Megan heard her voice wobble. "Just tell Jade I love her and I'll see her tomorrow."

"Is something wrong?" Anna asked, her voice suddenly tinged with worry. "You sound a little strange."

Sudden, unexpected tears clogged her throat. Damn it. She'd thought she had this under control.

"Everything's fine," she managed. "See you tomorrow."

After disconnecting, she looked around.

She was beginning to rethink her idea of staying in Coral Gables tonight. It might not be the first place Stephen thought to look for her, but it might occur to him if he reflected on it a bit.

With that thought, she strode purposely into her former bedroom and gathered up some clothes. She packed an ancient overnight bag.

She needed to ponder what to do, she thought, feeling sick to her stomach. This time, it would be hard for her to cut and run. She and Stephen were married, and there was a three-year-old child involved.

She knew he'd come after her—because of Jade, of course.

She couldn't believe she'd opened her heart to him again. *The jerk.*

She swung her overnight bag off the bed with more violence than necessary. *The philandering snake.*

This time, though, she decided her reaction would be different—not only because it had to be, but because she wanted it to be.

She walked toward the front door.

She wasn't going to be a passive victim. She wasn't meekly going away.

Outside, she locked up the house, tossed her overnight bag into the car, and got behind the wheel.

Jaw set, she knew exactly where she was going. First steps first.

She was checking into one of the Garrison Grand's rival hotels. It was just too bad the Hotel Victoria wasn't open yet.

Twelve

By the time Stephen got to the marina's parking lot, Megan was gone. Annoyed with himself for letting Tiffany slow him down, he whipped out his cell to try to reach Megan by phone.

When she didn't pick up then or on subsequent calls, he held out slim hope the reason was because she was driving. More likely, she'd drawn her own conclusions about the scenario that had apparently played out before her eyes.

He swore under his breath. He had to find her and fix this situation. He knew appearances were damning, but he had to convince her of the truth.

Just the thought she might walk away from him again made him nearly break out in a sweat.

He strode to his car, which was parked nearby. He was willing to do this the hard way—by process of elimination.

First, he headed to the most likely place he'd find her—his estate near South Beach.

When he didn't find her there, he grimly headed back out to his car. He decided to check his suite at the Garrison Grand next.

Before pulling out of his drive, however, he called Anna. It occurred to him Megan wouldn't do anything without making sure Jade was taken care of. Parker's wife might therefore be able to give him some leads.

When his sister-in-law picked up, he said, "Hi, Anna. Is Jade with you?"

"Yes, she's right here. I just got back from picking her up."

At least he knew where Jade was, Stephen thought, some of his tension easing. "Is Megan there?"

There was a pause on the line, and he could practically see Anna frowning.

"I thought she was with you," his sister-in-law said.

"There's been a…misunderstanding. Has she tried to contact you?"

"As a matter of fact, she did—"

Stephen's hand tightened on the phone.

"—but she didn't say where she was. She asked if I could keep Jade until tomorrow. Of course I said it was okay. I just stopped by your suite at the Garrison Grand on the way home and picked up some clothes for Jade."

Damn. Still, now he knew Megan wasn't at the hotel.

"Thanks, Anna," he said. "I'll be in touch. Give Jade a kiss for me."

"You know," Anna put in, "Megan said nearly the same thing when I talked to her. She wanted me to tell Jade she loved her."

At least, Stephen thought, there was one thing he and his wife agreed on at the moment. They were united in their love and concern for Jade.

"Are you sure everything is all right?" Anna asked.

"It will be soon," Stephen assured her.

When he ended the call, he sat and gazed down his driveway for a moment.

Now he knew Megan wasn't at the Garrison Grand, he was at loose ends. He'd covered the most logical bases, and Megan wasn't answering her phone.

He squinted into the distance, then realized there was one place he hadn't tried yet.

After turning the key in the ignition, he pulled away from the house and headed to Coral Gables.

Megan woke up disoriented.

She was in a strange room. A *hotel* room.

Then the drama of the previous evening came rushing back, and along with it, the queasy feeling there was no way to fix what was wrong with her life.

It was a feeling she'd had once before, when she'd found herself pregnant and alone, having realized the father of her child thought of her as nothing more than a fling.

Luckily, she'd found a hotel room yesterday. With the impending storm, there had been a number of last-minute cancellations of weekend reservations.

While she'd been tossing and turning in bed last night, she'd also come to a resolution.

The last time she'd caught Stephen cheating, she'd turned and run. She hadn't even sought an explanation from him. This time, though the evidence against him was damning, she wouldn't make the same mistake.

Now, after she showered, dressed and ate a light breakfast delivered by room service, she put in a call to Tiffany.

When the babysitter picked up, she announced without preamble, "You're fired."

"Megan?"

"Yes, it's me," she said crisply. "As of today, your services are no longer required."

"I can explain—"

"I'm sure you can," she responded, "but I don't want to hear it."

Afterward, she checked herself out of the hotel and headed for Stephen's estate.

She'd bolted, just like four years ago. But now, she was turning around and fighting.

Last night had to rank as the most miserable night of his life, Stephen reflected. Megan hadn't come home, and he hadn't been able to find her.

He poured himself another morning cup of coffee and paced back and forth in his kitchen.

He'd been up since six—not that he'd gotten much sleep. Though it was only late morning, he'd showered, dressed in jeans and a casual shirt, and been prowling around restlessly for what seemed like eons.

Yesterday, when he'd arrived at the house in Coral Gables, he'd discovered Megan wasn't there. However, he'd run into a neighbor who said she'd thought she'd seen Megan's car parked in front of the house not too long before.

Cursing his bad timing, but realizing he'd run out of options, he'd returned to his estate near South Beach.

Now, he looked outside at gray storm clouds and a steady rain.

Damn it. The storm was closing in, and if he didn't find Megan soon, he'd have to ride out the storm here—alone and without resolution.

The only silver lining was that Megan had asked

Anna to hold on to Jade only until today. That meant—at least he hoped it did—that Megan was bound to show up sooner rather than later.

He'd already phoned Anna this morning and told her to give him a call if Megan stopped by to pick up Jade. He'd sensed that his sister-in-law had questions but was refraining from asking them.

He knew Megan couldn't just take off this time. She had a partnership in her firm and a three-year-old who couldn't be uprooted easily. There was also a storm coming ashore. And most importantly, he'd find her—no matter how long it took—and make her see the truth.

Itching to do something *now,* however, he dialed the sitter. Perhaps Megan had contacted Tiffany. She'd seemed angry enough last night to let loose with some choice words aimed at the both of them.

When Tiffany picked up, he said, "It's Stephen. Have you heard from Megan?"

There was a pause. "You know, for no longer being in your employ," Tiffany drawled, "I sure do get a lot of calls from Garrisons."

Suddenly alert, he asked, "What do you mean you're no longer employed?"

"By you and your wife. She fired me."

Stephen felt his spirits lift, but he nevertheless asked sarcastically, "Even after your explanation that it was supposedly mutual?"

"It didn't get that far. She didn't even give me time to explain!"

At a sound behind him, he swung around and his eyes locked with Megan's.

"Talking to the other woman?" she asked, arching a brow.

"Gotta go, Tiffany," he said absently, then disconnected. He stared at Megan, willing her to be more than a figment of his imagination.

She looked like a mermaid that had been washed ashore and up to his doorstep. She was wearing a rain-splattered flower-print sundress, the shoulder straps of which cleverly continued beneath her breasts, outlining them. Her long red hair hung down her back, drops of rain reflecting the light cast by the overhead in the kitchen.

The way she looked right now, she took him back four years. Back to when she was still willing to play the seductress and he was her eager victim. Back to when things had been right between them.

He fought the urge to grab her and pull her into his arms. He settled for setting down the phone and walking toward her. "I didn't know where you were."

"Then let me put your mind at ease," she said, planting her handbag on a nearby chair. "The Tides Hotel."

Ouch. "You know how to hit a guy when he's down, don't you?"

"Funny, I thought I was the one who was down, and you—" her eyes went to his crotch "—were the one who was up."

She was taking no prisoners, he thought with an inner grimace. Still, ridiculously, he felt turned on.

"I thought you were going to bolt like before," he said.

"Can't." She shrugged and held up her hand. "I'm married to you this time."

He was close enough to glimpse uncertainty beneath her cool reserve, and he pressed forward. "I'm not letting you go."

Her eyes flashed. "You strong-armed me into this marriage—"

"Damn right, I did."

"I fired Tiffany."

"But you can't fire me."

"But I can divorce you," she said, her chin coming up.

His jaw set. *Like hell.*

"Were you carrying on with her?" she asked.

The question hung in the air between them. "Would you believe me if I said no?"

"Would any reasonable person?" she tossed back.

"I'm not giving you a divorce," he said implacably, "so forget it."

Megan watched the man she loved walk toward her, and held her breath.

His eyes were like hot coals, belying an expression carved in granite.

Yet beneath his hard, uncompromising attitude, she sensed a hint of vulnerability, and her heart somersaulted.

"I fired Tiffany before she gave me an explanation," she said.

He nodded. "I know. She told me. Why?"

"Maybe I learned from my mistakes," she said in a low voice. "Maybe I decided this time that if I was going to exact payment, it should fall on both guilty parties."

He nodded. "*Maybe,* but is that the real reason?"

He stopped in front of her, and she shook her head slowly, holding his gaze.

Her lips parted. "I didn't want an explanation. I was talking to Anna recently, and she mentioned the issue of *trust.* It's what was lacking the last time in our relationship. I like to think I learn from my mistakes."

"It looks bad—"

"Incriminating. So incriminating, in fact," she said, "that after the initial shock, I realized no one could be that stupid."

His face relaxed, his shoulders lowering.

"Who'd try to have a romantic encounter on his yacht when he knew his wife was due to meet him there soon?"

"When he'd gone to all the trouble of strong-arming the same wife into marrying him," he supplied.

"Exactly." She'd thought this through the night before—when she'd had a chance to calmly assess what had happened.

"I'm getting rid of *Fishful Thinking*," he said hoarsely.

Her eyes widened. "But you love that boat."

He stepped forward. "I love you more."

A crazy joy swept through her.

He raised his hand and pushed hair away from her face. "The yacht doesn't suit my lifestyle now, but there's an acquaintance who's expressed interest in buying it on more than one occasion."

His lips quirked in the lopsided smile that she'd always loved. "He used to be a rival of mine in Miami's playboy sweepstakes."

"You don't say," she said, a teasing tone creeping into her voice.

"I'm also stepping away from being the public face of the Garrison Grand."

She went still. "*What?* You can't do that."

"I can and I will," he responded, looking at her tenderly. "I don't need to be partying when what I really want is to be home."

It was a grand gesture, and sudden tears choked her.

"Are you going to say it?" he asked. "Because I'm prepared to wage a campaign if I have to."

"I love you!" She flung the words at him, even her vision blurred. "There, I said it. Are you happy now? You arrogant, ruthless—"

He yanked her into his arms. "I'm all those things and worse," he muttered, "but I love you."

Then he silenced her with a kiss. He didn't ask, he took, and they both gave themselves up to the kiss with wild abandon.

She'd taken the long way, she thought, but she finally had what she'd been looking for.

When his lips eventually moved away from hers, he trailed kisses along her cheek and to the hollow of her throat.

"You know," she joked breathlessly, her heart feeling lighter than it had in years, "if this keeps happening, I'm going to have to lock you up to keep women away from you."

"Don't worry, Meggikins," he said, his fingers searching for the zipper to her dress, "I intend to become the most family-oriented guy around. I want more kids, and I'm definitely going to enjoy making them."

She pretended to look shocked. "We can't spend all our time in bed!"

As if in response, he nuzzled her neck.

"Is this how men communicate their feelings?" she teased, her breath catching.

"What can I say? I'm a man of action."

His response elicited an involuntary laugh, even as he nibbled along her shoulder, sending waves of lush desire through her.

"We need to pick up Jade from Anna's before this storm really hits," he said reluctantly, kissing the tops of her breasts.

"Mmm," she responded. "I called Anna and Parker right before I got here. They're bringing over Jade shortly."

"In that case, we'll have to hurry."

Another laugh escaped her. "At this rate, I'll be pregnant in a month."

He raised his head to look at her seriously. "We talked about it in an 'if it happens' sort of way, but we can wait if you want to."

She shook her head. "I don't want to. Jade is going to be four, and I'd like her to have a sibling or two before she gets too much older. Now I'm a partner at Elkind, Ross, I've got some leverage as far as organizing my work schedule and taking a leave. I'll just have to space my projects further apart."

He smiled. "You'll have no problem getting clearance from your current client."

Then he lifted her onto the nearby kitchen table, bunching her dress around her hips in the process.

"The kitchen table—?"

"We haven't used it yet. Let's tick it off our list."

She slid back on her elbows to keep her balance. He was aroused, and she was weak-kneed.

"It's been one of my fantasies for a long time," he admitted, grasping her hips to pull the panties off her.

"How long?" she asked throatily.

"Too damn long," he responded. "Since you left."

She watched as he divested himself of some clothing. "Ah, those fantasies of yours…"

He looked at her, passion dilating his eyes. "We're about to make one of them come true."

"I'd dream about you, too, you know. I couldn't stop myself."

He stilled, looking at her. "Oh, yeah?"

His pose was all male swagger, tinged with hunger. She nodded.

He smiled. "Care to share?"

She shook her head. Just the thought made her—

"You're blushing." He leaned forward with wicked intent, bracing his arms on either side of her. "I'll just have to make you—"

"Nothing will make me spill my secrets," she said on a breathless laugh.

But he was already tracing a hot path to her cleavage, making her gasp.

"Whisper them to me…"

And she did, as they had grinding, pulse-throbbing sex on the kitchen table.

Later, as they were straightening their clothes, Stephen said, "After you saw Tiffany kissing me on the yacht, I thought I'd lost you for good."

"Was *she* kissing *you?*"

He nodded.

Megan was glad for the confirmation that her faith hadn't been misplaced. "I overheard you on the phone asking Tiffany about her explanation that it was supposedly mutual."

His lips twisted. "Yeah, that's her story, and she's sticking to it."

"It wouldn't have mattered," she responded. "I'd already made up my mind, but accidentally hearing your part of the phone conversation earlier was nice validation."

Stephen shook his head. "She's fairly savvy for a mixed-up kid."

Megan wondered whether she'd missed some signs where the babysitter was concerned. "I hired her through a child-care agency. She was available to babysit during the hours I needed because she's an aspiring dancer and attends classes in the evenings."

"Well, I'll be around to help now," Stephen said. "We'll continue adjusting our schedules to accommodate Jade, and I'll hire a live-in housekeeper. When I was a single guy, I didn't feel the need for permanent staff, but that's changed now."

She thought about Stephen's statement earlier. "I don't want you to give up the yacht for me."

"Not for you. For us."

"But we'll need *Fishful Thinking* to entertain all those kids you're planning to have," she teased.

He looked at her for a moment, then slipped his hands around her waist. "Do you know how much I love you?"

"Tell me again," she said, smiling as she placed her hands on his chest.

He gave her a quick kiss. "I don't think I ever got over you."

"Definitely likewise," she responded.

"You were right, you know," he added. "Until you walked away, I'd never had the experience of being dumped. It was a bitter pill, especially since I'd been crazy about you."

Her heart swelled. "Walking away from you was one of the hardest things I've ever done, even though I believed at the time that you'd cheated."

"I got a necessary dose of humility," he admitted. "After that, I toned down the playboy lifestyle and focused on building up the Garrison Grand."

"And got wonderful results for it," she said. "The Garrison Grand is considered the premier hotel in South Beach."

"Thanks, but I consider my greatest accomplishment to be Jade."

Her heart spilled over. "I feel the same way," she said softly.

He gave her a lingering kiss. "You hold my heart in your hands. You always have."

She raised her hand and stroked his face. "I never would have guessed. You looked so forbidding the day you walked into my office at Elkind, Ross."

"I was angry," he said, giving her a lopsided smile, "but I was determined to get you back in my bed."

"Oh?" She arched a brow.

"No woman has turned me on as much as you do," he said. "I was determined to reignite our affair and break it off only when I wanted to this time. Of course, I wasn't yet admitting to myself that time might be *never.*"

"Silly man," she said, her eyes misting. "So desperate, you had to blackmail me into marrying you."

"Not one of my finer moments," he admitted. "I wanted to believe I was in control, but the reality was the opposite."

He was laying himself bare for her, and joy bubbled up inside her again. Before either of them could say anything else, however, the doorbell rang.

"Jade," she said.

Stephen nodded. "I'll get it."

Moments later, he walked back into the kitchen, trailing an exuberant Jade. Parker and Anna followed behind.

"Mommy!" Jade rushed forward, and Megan bent and wrapped her daughter in her arms.

"I played board games with Aunt Anna and Uncle Parker! And I got ice cream! And Gillian's party was great, and—"

Everyone laughed.

"Slow down there," Stephen said, ruffling Jade's hair.

Megan watched as Anna looked at her, a question in her eyes.

"Is everything okay?" Anna asked, her gaze going from her to Stephen.

"Perfect now," Megan said.

Stephen slipped his arm around her and pulled Jade close to him with his other.

Megan smiled at Anna, trying to communicate that everything truly was fine now. The message seemed to come across because, after a moment, her sister-in-law smiled back and squeezed Parker's hand.

"Now that I've been to Gillian's house, I know what I want!" Jade piped up.

"What?" she and Stephen asked in unison.

"A little brother or sister," Jade announced, then ducked under Stephen's arm and skipped away. "*I* get to tell them what to do!"

Megan felt herself heat, and Stephen laughed.

Anna and Parker looked amused but knowing.

"Uh-oh," Stephen said. "I think we're in trouble."

"She's definitely *your* daughter," Megan teased, looking up at him with her heart in her eyes, "and we've definitely come home to stay."

* * * * *

Desire

There was only one man for the job—
an impossible-to-resist maverick
she knew she didn't dare fall for.

MAVERICK
(#1827)

BY *NEW YORK TIMES*
BESTSELLING AUTHOR
JOAN HOHL

"Will You Do It for One Million Dollars?"

Any other time, Tanner Wolfe would have balked at being
hired by a woman. Yet Brianna Stewart was desperate to
engage the infamous bounty hunter. The price was just
high enough to gain Tanner's interest…Brianna's beauty
definitely strong enough to keep it. But he wasn't about
to allow her to tag along on his mission. He worked
alone. Always had. Always would. However, he'd never
confronted a more determined client than Brianna. She
wasn't taking no for an answer—not about anything.

Perhaps a million-dollar bounty was not the only thing
this maverick was about to gain….

Look for MAVERICK

Available October 2007 wherever you buy books.

Mediterranean NIGHTS™

Sail aboard the luxurious Alexandra's Dream and experience glamour, romance, mystery and revenge!

Coming in October 2007...

AN AFFAIR TO REMEMBER

by

Karen Kendall

When Captain Nikolas Pappas first fell in love with Helena Stamos, he was a penniless deckhand and she was the daughter of a shipping magnate. But he's never forgiven himself for the way he left her—and fifteen years later, he's determined to win her back.

Though the attraction is still there, Helena is hesitant to get involved. Nick left her once...what's to stop him from doing it again?

www.eHarlequin.com

HM38964

REQUEST YOUR FREE BOOKS!

2 FREE NOVELS
PLUS 2
FREE GIFTS!

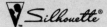

Passionate, Powerful, Provocative!

YES! Please send me 2 FREE Silhouette Desire® novels and my 2 FREE gifts. After receiving them, if I don't wish to receive any more books, I can return the shipping statement marked "cancel." If I don't cancel, I will receive 6 brand-new novels every month and be billed just $3.80 per book in the U.S., or $4.47 per book in Canada, plus 25¢ shipping and handling per book and applicable taxes, if any*. That's a savings of almost 15% off the cover price! I understand that accepting the 2 free books and gifts places me under no obligation to buy anything. I can always return a shipment and cancel at any time. Even if I never buy another book from Silhouette, the two free books and gifts are mine to keep forever.   225 SDN EEXJ 326 SDN EEXU

Name	(PLEASE PRINT)

Address	Apt.

City	State/Prov.	Zip/Postal Code

Signature (if under 18, a parent or guardian must sign)

Mail to the **Silhouette Reader Service**™:
IN U.S.A.: P.O. Box 1867, Buffalo, NY 14240-1867
IN CANADA: P.O. Box 609, Fort Erie, Ontario L2A 5X3

Not valid to current Silhouette Desire subscribers.

Want to try two free books from another line?
Call 1-800-873-8635 or visit www.morefreebooks.com.

* Terms and prices subject to change without notice. NY residents add applicable sales tax. Canadian residents will be charged applicable provincial taxes and GST. This offer is limited to one order per household. All orders subject to approval. Credit or debit balances in a customer's account(s) may be offset by any other outstanding balance owed by or to the customer. Please allow 4 to 6 weeks for delivery.

Your Privacy: Silhouette is committed to protecting your privacy. Our Privacy Policy is available online at www.eHarlequin.com or upon request from the Reader Service. From time to time we make our lists of customers available to reputable firms who may have a product or service of interest to you. If you would prefer we not share your name and address, please check here. ☐

SDES07

nocturne™

Look for

NIGHT MISCHIEF

by

NINA BRUHNS

Lady Dawn Maybank's worst nightmare
is realized when she accidentally conjures
a demon of vengeance, Galen McManus. What
she doesn't realize is that Galen plans to teach
her a lesson in love—one she'll never forget....

DARK
ENCHANTMENTS

▲

Available October wherever you buy books.

Don't miss the last installment of Dark Enchantments,
SAVING DESTINY by Pat White, available November.

ATHENA FORCE

Heart-pounding romance and thrilling adventure.

A deadly masquerade

As an undercover asset for the FBI, mafia princess Sasha Bracciali can deceive and improvise at a moment's notice. But when she's cut off from everything she knows, including her FBI-agent lover, Sasha realizes her deceptions have masked a painful truth: she doesn't know whom to trust. If she doesn't figure it out quickly, her most ambitious charade will also be her last.

Look for

CHARADE
by *Kate Donovan*

Available in October wherever you buy books.

Ria Sterling has the gift—or is it a curse?—
of seeing a person's future in his or her
photograph. Unfortunately, when detective
Carrick Jones brings her a missing person's
case, she glimpses his partner's ID—and
sees imminent murder. And when her vision
comes true, Ria becomes the prime suspect.
Carrick isn't convinced this beautiful woman
committed the crime...but does he believe
she has the special powers to solve it?

Look for

Seeing Is Believing

by

Kate Austin

Available October
wherever you buy books.

COMING NEXT MONTH

SDCNM0907